Velvet
Snowflakes

Velvet Snowflakes

BARBARA BRIGGS WARD

Published by Wheatmark®
2030 East Speedway Boulevard, Suite 106
Tucson, Arizona 85719 USA
www.wheatmark.com

ISBN: 978-1-62787-979-8 (paperback)
ISBN: 978-1-62787-980-4 (ebook)
LCCN: 2022908922

Bulk ordering discounts are available through Wheatmark, Inc. For more information, email orders@wheatmark.com or call 1-888-934-0888.

Home remains in one's heart forever

Chapter One

"Ivy Nolan is a visionary designer. Fabric is her tool" was the headline in the *New York Times*.

On a Monday evening in early December, Ivy Nolan, named Wedding Gown Designer of the Year at the annual gala of industry leaders held at the Plaza in November, was on a train heading north, back to where she grew up. Since the gala, Ivy realized her success was due in part to three strangers who came into her life at varied moments, just when she needed them. That's why she was on the train. She was returning to thank them. Problem was, Ivy had no clue if they were still around. Or still alive. Having focused on building her brand in such a competitive field, she'd lost touch with that other world she left behind after her twenty-first birthday.

That was seventeen years ago.

Ivy had called the caretaker of her property to let him know what time she would be arriving. Along with parking her truck at the train depot, he'd have everything taken care of, including getting her groceries and putting them away.

With Christmas less than three weeks away, she decided to stay a week, depending on what she found once she got there. A charity event coming up in early January meant her time was limited. It took a lot of work to prepare for the yearly event in the city, but it was worth it. The money raised helped many in need.

Ivy's property was located outside the village. A Dutch-style barn and outhouses were included. When buying the property, her plan had been to own a few horses, maybe even some sheep or chickens, but those plans were still way down the road. Ivy never seemed to find the time to get back there and when she did, Ivy was like a hermit. She loved the quiet.

The stillness woke Ivy up the next morning. She'd had a good sleep. She always did when back in the old farmhouse. Looking out the window, the view took her breath away. Watching the wind carry snow across a field reminded Ivy of the emerald-green velvet wedding gown she'd submitted to the panel of judges responsible for selecting the Designer of the Year. Ivy named it the Winter Gown. Velvet fit the season. While it was the only velvet gown in the mix, it wasn't the first velvet gown she'd designed. Just thinking about the night she wore that first gown gave her a headache.

Showered and dressed, with her auburn hair pulled up in a ponytail and a cup of coffee in hand, Ivy sat down at the kitchen table. Her plan was to write a note to each of those three people. Since she didn't have addresses, Ivy would personally deliver the notecards to where they'd first met. She'd thought about them when riding on the train. That made writing the personal notes easier.

It also made her realize that despite all her success, something was missing.

Chapter Two

OLD MAN NEXT DOOR

His name was Doc Armstrong. Ivy never knew his first name, but then she was only a little girl. He lived next door in what she remembered was a large house with a wide front porch. That's where Ivy spent many summer afternoons playing checkers with him while her younger sister, Izzie, played with her favorite dolls. On most of those afternoons, Doc would go inside and return with lemonade served in juice glasses for the three of them. He kept candy bars in his sweater pocket to share with the girls.

Sometimes they'd go with him down the lane to his small barn. As they walked inside, Doc would always say, "Don't touch the animals. Some don't feel very good today."

Doc was a veterinarian. Ivy never cared if the barn wasn't full of animals. A dog or cat or bunny was fine.

At one point, when the girls were leaving to go home, Doc began telling them, "Be sure to help your mother. She's doing the best she can."

Eventually Ivy realized he was telling them to be kind to their mother because their father had moved out. Sometimes, in the middle of the night, Ivy could hear her crying or shouting at her father over the phone. Her mother was a nurse. She worked the evening shift. Now instead of their father being there in the evening, an older girl babysat Ivy and her sister.

On the first Christmas Eve following the divorce, the babysitter never showed up, and their mother had to go to work.

"Doc would babysit," Ivy suggested. "I know he would."

Her mother had no choice.

"Don't worry about us," Doc Armstrong said as he came through the kitchen door wearing a Santa Claus hat. "We'll have lots of fun."

He turned out to be a wonderful babysitter. Together they baked sugar cookies and decided which ones to leave for Santa with a glass of milk. Then the girls picked out their favorite Christmas stories. Sitting between them on a sofa near a small Christmas tree, Doc read to them. After that, he made a suggestion.

"Let's make your mommy and daddy Christmas cards."

"But Daddy doesn't live here anymore."

"He's still your daddy. He always will be, Ivy."

"Mommy will get mad if we make Daddy a card."

"Your mommy knows how much you both love your daddy. I can tell that makes her happy."

Out came the crayons and paper. Soon they were hiding their homemade Christmas cards. They couldn't wait to surprise their parents. But the biggest surprise came when Doc Armstrong told the girls to get their snowsuits on. They were going outside.

"Button up. I must check the animals sleeping in the barn."

Ivy helped Izzie with her coat.

As they were going out the door, Doc threw a pillowcase with stuff in it over his shoulder.

"What's in there?" Izzie asked.

"'Tis Christmas Eve, my littlest one. The night of surprises."

It was snowing. Lightly, magically snowing. Crunching under their boots snowing.

"Before we visit the animals," Doc explained as he went into the barn and brought out an old cutter sitting by the door. "I thought

I'd take you two on a sleigh ride. Climb in, girls. We'll go around the block."

It was a red cutter with a high handle on the back.

Once Ivy and Izzie were settled, Doc covered them up with blankets and began pushing the cutter down the lane.

The stars were glistening between the snowflakes.

"It's a beautiful Christmas Eve," he remarked.

As they went along, Doc told the girls a story about a Christmas Eve long ago.

"I was around your age, Ivy. It didn't feel like Christmas. My mother was quite sick. She was in the hospital. My big brother baby-sat me and my sisters while our father went to see our mother. We didn't have a Christmas tree. We never made Santa cookies. No stockings were hung or presents bought. I went to bed and cried myself to sleep. When I woke up, I could smell the kind of muffins my mother always baked on Christmas morning. I got my brother and sisters up and we ran downstairs. My mother was still sick. My father was still at the hospital. But Uncle Art was in the kitchen. He was the one making the Christmas muffins. Aunt Mary was putting a tiny little tree with tiny little decorations on the dining room table. Although we didn't have any presents that year, we did sit around the table with the tiny little tree and eat lots of those muffins. They tasted just like our mother's. Then Uncle Art made giant pancakes. He put funny faces on them using raisins, banana slices, apple slices, little mints, and chocolate chips. Later we cut out Christmas cookies with Aunt Mary, and after that we went outside and made snowmen. When our father came home and told us our mother was getting better, that was the best present ever."

The trip around the block was a quick one, ending just as Doc finished his story.

"Let's check the animals," he said, smiling.

Going into the barn, the girls were excited to find kittens and a bunny and three puppies all sound asleep. But it was a little reindeer with bells around her neck that brought the most excitement.

"This is Scarlett. She's too little to go with Santa, so he asked if she could stay for a while."

"When is Santa picking her up?" Ivy asked.

"He'll be back when you are sleeping."

Being in the old barn on a snowy Christmas Eve with the little reindeer and Doc Armstrong resembling Santa, with his white hair and beard and a twinkle in his eyes, and the old red cutter, the kittens, the bunny, the puppies, the cookies and candy canes wrapped up on a paper plate Doc pulled out of the pillowcase, along with the sweetest decorations to put around the barn, all blended together in a moment Ivy would never forget as she grew up to be a creator of wedding gowns—each gown influenced by the wonder she felt on that Christmas Eve. Without that wonder, Ivy's wedding gowns would have been just more wedding gowns bunched together, hanging on racks inside stores full of racks.

Ivy's note to Doc was magical: *Thank you for instilling within me the wonder of Christmas in every gown I create.*

FABRIC SHOP LADY

When Ivy was in the first semester of her second year at a community college about an hour from where she lived, a few girls asked her to go with them to a home football game at a private university in the same community. Ivy hadn't had much of a social life up until then.

"It should be lots of fun," one of the girls explained.

It turned out to be fun. So much fun.

When the home team won, the crowd went wild. Strangers were hugging strangers in the stands. It was a hint of English Leather and her cheek resting on a fine woolen sweater while wrapped up in arms holding her close that made Ivy look up into eyes as blue as the October sky. The warm afternoon sun was not the reason Ivy was overwhelmed. It was the young man hugging her. When he smiled and introduced himself, Ivy was hooked.

"Hi, beautiful. I'm John. I don't want to let you go."

From then on, the two were together every possible moment. John was in his junior year at the university. In late November he asked Ivy to be his date for their annual Holiday Ball. Following tradition, it would be held the week before Christmas at the historic downtown Grand Hotel, with a winding front porch and a fireplace in every room. The hotel was located in Ivy's hometown, known for its restored turn-of-the-century buildings.

"It's nothing like the Plaza, but it will do," John remarked.

A native of New York, he was always referencing the city in conversations. Ivy had never been there.

"I've reserved us a room overlooking the river," he told her a few days later. "It comes with a king-size bed and all the champagne we can drink."

Ivy knew what that meant. She couldn't wait. It would be a night to remember, especially with John leaving for Christmas vacation the next day. A friend of Ivy's was going to the ball as well. She'd gone the year before.

"It's quite the ritzy evening, Ivy. I didn't dress as elegantly as I should have last year. I'll make up for it this time. Mom and I are going out of town shopping for a dress this weekend if you'd like to come along."

"I'll think about it," Ivy replied, knowing she wouldn't be joining them. She had an idea. On Saturday morning she went shopping. All by herself.

Ivy knew where she was going.

The shop was located on a side street close to downtown. When Ivy opened the door, a small bell announced her arrival. A few women were sitting at a table looking through some catalogs. Seconds later an older woman came in from a back room to greet her.

"Welcome. My name is Vivian. I own the shop. I'm helping these women now, but as soon as I'm finished, I'll be right with you. Did you have anything particular in mind?"

Ivy explained she was going to the ball.

"What gave you the idea that you'd prefer your gown to be sewn? That's quite the classy affair."

"My grandmother was a seamstress. I loved watching her sew one-of-a-kind, fancy dresses. I want my dress to be a gown, exclusively mine. I have some ideas."

From that point on, Ivy spent whatever time she could in the fabric shop. The two formed a close relationship despite their age difference.

"Even though your hair is a caramel blond and my grandmother's was silver-gray, you remind me of her. She too wore a tape measure around her neck and straight pins on her sleeve," Ivy told Vivian one morning.

"I guess we seamstresses are all the same. We need everything close by once the creating begins."

As they moved along in the process, Vivian became a teacher of fabric and design and cutting out patterns. She talked about netting and lace. Explained the differences in various evening gown materials. Every piece of information Vivian offered; Ivy wrote down in a notebook. When Vivian pulled out a bolt of plush velvet, Ivy became infatuated. Of course, it was snowing out and the thought of being with John in that hotel, dancing in his arms and later sipping champagne and making love, all came at her at once as she imagined wearing a flowing emerald-green velvet gown exclusively her own.

With pencil in hand, Ivy became a designer. When finished with her evening gown sketch, she showed Vivian.

"With the off-the-shoulder line, long, snug sleeves, and flowing skirt to the floor, this gown will be elegant. It reminds me of the glory days of Hollywood. You have an eye for design, young lady."

Taking Ivy's measurements, the seamstress went to work making pattern pieces. A few days later, Ivy had her first fitting. All that was needed was the hemming. Then Vivian sent it to the cleaners along with a matching velvet evening bag. She'd embroidered little cranberry hearts around the bottom. She didn't tell Ivy about the evening bag. She wanted to surprise her.

Ivy's note to Vivian was creative: *Thank you for infusing within me a respect for fine fabrics and a heart and eye for designing wedding gowns sewn with love.*

HOTEL MANAGER

John and Ivy checked into their room at the downtown Grand Hotel early.

"What do you say we skip the ball? Stay here. Enjoy some bubbly and each other."

"We'll have all night," Ivy replied, taking hold of her gown and shoes.

Instead of complimenting Ivy on how beautiful she looked once she was ready to go, John began kissing her. Then he tried unzipping her gown.

"Anticipation, Johnny. Let's go dancing. Then you can unzip me."

"You're such a tease, Ivy. I love it!"

"Oh, wait. I forgot the evening bag Vivian surprised me with the other day."

Ivy looked everywhere. She couldn't find it.

"Would you run down and look outside? Maybe I dropped it on the porch or in the snow. I'll check around the room again. It has little cranberry hearts around the bottom."

"I'm not going looking for a bag with little hearts. I can think of better things we could be doing."

John had her in his grip again, going for the zipper.

Ivy pushed him away.

"I said later, John."

Ivy opened the door. "Well, come on. The sooner we go, the sooner we'll get back."

"Oh, you know how to turn me on, Ivy. I'll get the gown unzipped in seconds. Then the real fun will begin."

John never did unzip the gown. As the band played the last slow dance of the evening in the lavishly decorated ballroom, he whispered, "After tonight, I won't be seeing you again, so let's get upstairs."

Ivy pulled away.

"What are you saying, John?"

"I've wanted to tell you, but I didn't know how."

"Tell me what?"

"I'll tell you upstairs," he whispered, holding her, kissing her. "Let's go."

"No!" Again, Ivy pulled away, shouting. "Tell me right here."

"Quiet down, Ivy."

"I won't quiet down. Tell me!"

"Okay! When I go home tomorrow, I won't be coming back, so I suggest you come with me. Now."

Ivy ignored him.

"What's her name, John?"

"What do you mean?"

"You know what I mean."

"Linda."

"Do you love Linda?"

"We're getting married."

"Get your stuff. Pay for the room, then leave."

"You know you want me, Ivy. Let's take care of business. I'm out of here early in the morning."

"You're leaving now!"

Ivy's friends surrounded her.

"You could have had some fun, Ivy girl." John laughed, running up the stairs.

Minutes later he was gone. Ivy hurried to the room. With her gown still on, she threw herself on the bed and began sobbing, eventually falling asleep. Waking up around two, Ivy changed her clothes. Tossing the green velvet gown into the trash, Ivy put her coat on and hurried down the stairs and out the door.

Standing there with the snow falling, Ivy had no clue what to do. Noticing a swing at one end of the porch, she went over and sat down. It was covered in snow. Ivy didn't care. A few minutes later, the door opened and a gentleman in a fine Italian woolen suit walked toward her. Ivy never noticed. When he spoke to her softly, it was as if an angel had come to her rescue.

"May I be of assistance, Miss?"

"No. No." Ivy cleared her throat. "No, I was just leaving."

"My name is Murphy. I manage the hotel. Before you go, would you like to come back inside and have a cup of hot chocolate with me? I saw you dancing earlier with a young man. Now I find you out here alone. I thought maybe you'd like to talk. It's none of my business, of course. At least come in out of the cold."

Ivy surprised herself by saying yes to the hot chocolate. A few minutes later, the two were sitting at a table in the middle of the grand ballroom sipping hot chocolate and talking as if they were old friends. Only the kitchen staff and a few others were around. With a tender smile, hints of red hair, and an ear for listening, Murphy helped Ivy make sense of the evening. She told him everything.

"I don't know what I did wrong. I thought we'd be together forever."

"Other than in the movies, there's no forever guarantee, Ivy."

"But he promised."

"I promised my little girl, Angela, I'd be home for dinner, and I wasn't."

"Dinner and a lifetime commitment are two different things."

"Not to my daughter."

"I wonder if John really cared for me. Think so?"

"I never knew the guy, but from what you've told me, he sounds like a spoiled brat."

"His family has money."

"I meet all kinds of people, Ivy. What I notice first is their smile, if they have one. Then I look for their kindness. I heard you speaking kindly to the waitress who spilled water at your table earlier. No one needs money to smile or be kind. They both take heart. You have heart, Ivy. You also have talent. I understand you designed that gorgeous gown you were wearing. John's rejection will become your blessing. Keep designing."

"You think I could be a designer?"

"You already are. You were getting compliments throughout the evening."

"Not from John."

"That's not in his character. People like John are used to having control because of their wealth. But you're the one who took control on the dance floor. You put him in his place. You have what it takes to make it with whatever you decide to design."

"It would be wedding gowns."

"Envision those gowns. Every day tell yourself you are a designer. That velvet gown marks the beginning of your journey. It is your Picasso." When they finished their hot chocolate, Murphy gave Ivy a ride home. Ivy never mentioned her velvet gown was upstairs in a trash can in his grand hotel.

Ivy's note to Murphy was grateful: *Thank you for taking me in out of the cold and warming me up with hot chocolate served with kindness.*

With the three notecards ready to go, Ivy set out to deliver them.

Chapter Three

THE HISTORIC DOWNTOWN GRAND HOTEL WAS Ivy's first stop. From what she could see, it hadn't aged. With the snow falling and a familiar swing moving in the breeze, Ivy's thoughts went back to that night and that dance and John. But only for a moment. She didn't recognize that version of herself anymore, in awe of a young man's looks and nice clothes and wealthy family and connections. Every time he'd reference the city, Ivy would feel limited and unworthy, thankful to be hanging on his arm and hopefully lucky enough to be another toy in his bed.

That was all behind her.

Now when Ivy expressed any doubt about her capabilities, her loyal assistant would put her back on track. Lawrence had been with Ivy since the beginning of her journey.

Walking up the steps of the winding front porch, she thought about that swing.

"I wonder how many other rejected souls have sat there," Ivy thought as she entered the hotel, decorated as splendidly as it was the only other time she'd been there.

An important-looking woman dressed in a black suit and pearls with a nametag telling Ivy her name was Monica stood behind the front desk.

"Good day and welcome. How may I help you?"

Ivy told her she was there to see Murphy.

"Murphy is president of marketing working out of our corporate headquarters in Chicago. I'll try his direct line."

A few seconds later, Murphy and Ivy were connected.

"Do you remember me, Murphy?"

"I've never forgotten you, Ivy."

"You rescued me that awful night. You made a difference in my life."

"Thank you, Ivy. Sometimes we're in the right place at the right time for a reason. I don't think I've ever enjoyed hot chocolate more than I did that night. Congratulations on all you have achieved!"

"Thanks, Murphy. Next time I'm in Chicago, we'll have dinner and catch up."

"How long will you be back home visiting?"

"I planned on possibly a week, but we'll see. Maybe more. Maybe less."

"My wife and I will be there for the holidays. I'm not sure exactly when. We'll be staying at my brother's, although he doesn't know it. He's turning seventy the day after Christmas, and the family is throwing him a surprise party."

"I'll give you my cell phone number. Maybe we can connect."

"That would be wonderful. I must tell you, Ivy, my daughter, Angela, is getting married next summer. She and my wife went shopping for the wedding gown a few weeks ago and that gown turned out to be one of yours. I'm not allowed to see even a photo of the gown, but they both continue to rave about it."

"I'm so happy one of my designs will be worn by your daughter. Is this the daughter you promised you'd be home for dinner but never made it?"

"Yes. Angela is my only daughter. I'm surprised you remember me telling you that."

"I remember everything from that night."

"We all have moments that can make us or break us. I dare say that night was a turning point for you in a positive way."

"It took me a few days to get beyond being dumped in front of

14

so many people. I was totally embarrassed. I felt like a piece of trash. The only good thing that came from being with that loser was his constant mentioning of New York. I became intrigued with the city. I did some searching and discovered the Fashion Institute and never looked back."

"My daughter showed me your website. I know nothing about your industry, but I do value fine fabric. Your gowns are exquisite."

"Thanks, Murphy. When you and I were sitting in that grand ballroom drinking our hot chocolate, I noticed your suit. It was a fine Italian woolen material."

"That was the most comfortable suit I've ever worn."

Plans were made to get back in touch once their holiday schedules were finalized.

Ivy left Murphy's note with Monica, who'd send it out by courier.

Chapter Four

Next on Ivy's list was Vivian's fabric shop.

When she opened the door, the little bell above it announced her presence. A young lady was cutting fabric.

"Good day," she smiled. "May I help you?"

About to reply, Ivy noticed someone using a cane coming toward her. That someone had caramel-blond hair.

"Vivian! Vivian, it's me, Ivy!"

Tears fell as they embraced, laughing, overjoyed as the bell over the door announced the arrival of another customer.

"I've got it, Vivian," said the young woman cutting fabric.

"Thank you, Maggie."

Taking hold of Ivy's hand, Vivian whispered, "Oh, my! How wonderful it is to see you! Let's go in the back. We can talk there and not be interrupted."

After some coffee and catching up, Vivian turned her attention to the cane by her side.

"About a year ago, some damn fool was going down a one-way the wrong way. It was icy. He was speeding and lost control of his vehicle. Came right up on the sidewalk and rammed into me. I was lucky. I only suffered a broken leg, a broken elbow, and some broken ribs."

"Vivian, I'm so sorry. How terrifying that must have been for you."

"You were a big help, Ivy."

"Me?"

"I recently received an email from an industry organization announcing you'd been selected Wedding Gown Designer of the Year. I burst into tears. I've followed your journey, Ivy. The moment that guy ran me over, I thought about you and your determination in such a highly competitive field and how you've kept pushing forward. That kept me moving forward when I didn't want to budge."

"You're the sweetest person I know, Vivian. Are you doing okay?"

"I'm getting stronger every day. But I do have a question."

"You can ask me anything."

"What was your inspiration for the Winter Gown? I read it was the only velvet gown submitted. It was stunning. The long, tapered sleeves with what looked like a rayon silk velvet brocade cuff was quite clever."

"Thank you, Vivian. To me, velvet made the most sense considering the time of year the judging would be taking place. The design of the dress took minutes. I'd been mulling it over in my head. You know how that goes."

"Yes, I do. Remember the fun we had creating your first velvet gown, the original Winter Gown? We were quite the team. Do you have someone helping you?"

"I do. He is invaluable."

"He?"

"Yes. Lawrence and I met at the Fashion Institute. One February afternoon, classes were canceled because of a blizzard. I was trying to make it to my apartment on foot, getting blown all over the place. That's when Lawrence drove past me. He came back, picked me up, and took me to his family's Italian restaurant. Despite being closed because of the storm, they cooked us a delicious meal."

"How romantic, Ivy! Damsel in distress is rescued by a young man who treats her to a fine Italian meal."

"It was more like two friends making the most of a New York City blizzard. Lawrence and I ended up enjoying his mother's tiramisu after the main course and a few bottles of wine. We sat there and talked for hours. While his interest was the business side, he encouraged me to keep designing. He told me I had a unique eye and said he wanted to work for me some day. Now he does, and I would be lost without him. We have a big charity event coming up in January, and he's taking care of all the little details."

"Do you mean little details such as publicity and ordering a caterer and flowers and so on?"

"Exactly! He makes it possible for me to only think of the gowns."

"Sounds like the perfect arrangement."

Aware of the time, Ivy took the written note from her pocket. "I came home to thank a few people who made a difference in my life. You, my dear Vivian, are one of those people. This card is simple. My love for you is forever."

"Thank you, Ivy. I can still see you walking through the door for the first time. You were curious. You asked questions and listened. It was obvious to me how uniquely talented you were. I simply made you see that as well."

Chapter Five

Ivy pulled up in front of Doc Armstrong's home early the following afternoon. Looking at her old house next door, now painted yellow with a yellow fence around it, she thought of her parents and Izzie. She hadn't heard much from them since going off to the Fashion Institute and from there to building her label and getting noticed. Last she knew her mother had moved to Florida. Her father had retired. Izzie was married.

Ivy didn't have time for wishing things were different.

Going up steps she'd gone up so many times before, Ivy pushed the doorbell. After waiting with no response, she went to the edge of the porch and looked down the lane. Doc's barn was still there. It looked even bigger. She could tell he was inside. A light was on.

"If the light over the front door is on, that means I'm there," Doc would tell people.

Walking by that yellow house, Ivy glanced up to what had been her bedroom window. She remembered the times she'd lay at the end of her bed looking out, watching Doc care for his animals. She remembered lying there crying, wondering why her daddy left. On the Christmas Eve following the Christmas Eve when Doc was the babysitter and surprised Ivy and Izzie with the little reindeer, Ivy had been lying on her bed looking over at Doc's home all decorated for the holidays. It was snowing. Sparkling tree lights were shining through the living room window as family gathered in celebration. There was no celebration in Ivy's house. No family gathered. No decorated tree reached the ceiling. Instead, a very small fake tree with decorations attached sat in the middle of the dining room table. A few wrapped gifts sat on the sofa. It was just Ivy, her sister, and their mother, who had the night off from work. She'd cooked the girls their favorite spaghetti and meatballs but fell asleep on the sofa after doing the dishes. Ivy helped Izzie hang her stocking. Then she brought Izzie upstairs and tucked her into bed, telling her to get to sleep because Santa was coming.

"But, Ivy, we didn't put cookies and milk out for Santa."

"Don't worry, Izzie. I'm going to do that after I get my pajamas on."

Ivy hoped she sounded convincing. Hurrying back down the stairs, she searched the cupboard for cookies. There were none. Way back on the last shelf, Ivy found a box of graham crackers. After crumbling one of the crackers to make it look like cookie crumbs, she put the plate with the crumbs and a small glass of milk on the counter. Then she turned the lights out and went to bed.

With the wonder of Christmas Eve streaming through the window by her bed, Ivy pushed her stuffed animals aside and climbed in under the covers. She tried ignoring the moon and the stars and Doc's two beautiful Christmas trees at either end of a bay window. But it was impossible. Christmas surrounded her. Sitting up, moving closer to her window, Ivy watched precious snowflakes swirl by on the most magical night of the year. Doc's family had gone home yet the Christmas lights were still on. Ivy felt so alone. Her family remained torn apart. Sitting in the dark, crying, Ivy noticed a little teddy bear lying on the floor. He looked as sad as Ivy felt. Picking him up and giving him a hug, Ivy sat him on the windowsill as more and more precious snowflakes fell. When carolers walked by singing "Silent Night", Ivy took hold of the sad little teddy bear. Pulling blankets around her, Ivy cried herself to sleep.

Her mother sold the house the following spring. Ivy had the hardest time saying goodbye to Doc. She never returned. Until now.

Ivy kept going down the lane. Snow was falling. She was surprised to see maybe seven or eight reindeer behind a fence that wasn't there when she was growing up. Neither was a smaller building with what looked like bales of hay stacked under a tarp. Hurrying inside the barn, Ivy noted the red cutter still in its place as were the sweetest decorations and more candy canes. She heard someone whistling. Doc Armstrong loved to whistle. It was coming from what Ivy remembered was a storage room. The door was half open. She didn't want to scare him, so she gently called out his name. On the third try, the whistling stopped. The door was pushed open even further.

"Oh, I'm sorry," Ivy said to a stranger. "I was looking for Doc Armstrong. Your whistling sounded just like his."

"That is a compliment," replied a rather tall man with a square chin and soft blue eyes like Doc's. Extending a hand, he introduced himself. "I'm Andy Armstrong."

"My name's Ivy Nolan. It's nice to meet you, Andy. I used to live next door, in the house now painted yellow. Are you a relative of Doc's? Does he still live here? Is he well?"

Instead of answering the questions, Andy Armstrong stood staring at Ivy before responding. "I remember seeing you on the front porch." He paused. "Please. Have a seat, Ivy. I'm Doc's grandson. I too am a veterinarian."

Ivy listened to a grandson talk about his grandfather.

"I was a shy kid. Sometimes when you were playing checkers with my grandfather, I was inside the house peeking through the curtains. My father was an only child. He died in a car accident when I was a young boy. My mother was teaching at the time, going to grad school nights. When she was in a pinch for a babysitter, my grandparents helped. My grandfather did most of it. After my grandmother passed away, it was just my grandfather in that big house unless I was sleeping over, which was quite often."

Ivy interrupted. "There's a rather large reindeer peering through the back window."

"That's Walter. He's quite nosy."

Ivy spoke about that Christmas Eve when Doc was the babysitter.

"After making cookies and reading books, your grandfather put my sister Izzie and me in his red cutter and took us for a walk around the block. It was snowing. It was magical. When we went inside the barn, we were excited to find a little reindeer with bells around her neck."

"Come with me, Ivy."

Andy led Ivy to a wall lined with cubbyholes.

"This wall is where my grandfather stores his most valuable possessions."

Getting up on a ladder, reaching into a cubbyhole near the top, he pulled out a leather evening bag.

"When I took over his practice, my grandfather pointed out a few things he wanted kept where they were. This evening bag was one of them."

As Andy opened the evening bag, Ivy heard the bells.

"Just hearing those bells takes me back to that Christmas Eve."

A For Sale sign distracted Ivy.

"Is this place for sale?"

"It's a long story."

"Is your grandfather okay?"

"He's in his eighties and remains in good health. He still fights like hell when he has to and lately, he's had to."

"What's going on?"

"I'll let my grandfather explain. I heard him pull up. He will be overjoyed to see you."

Standing there, waiting for the door to open, Andy whispered, "You know, Ivy, most kids would never have bothered with an old man and his stories."

"Hearing those bells fills me with gratitude. Doc remains the happiest story of my childhood."

Chapter Six

"Slow down, Walter. Hey! Watch where you're going! No treats if you step all over me. Look out! You'll be stepping on Pearl, too!"

Doc noticed Andy standing there. Then he noticed what he considered to be a stranger.

"Oh. So sorry. I wasn't aware you were with someone, Dr. Armstrong. Walter blatted when he saw me. Now he has Pearl upset. I'll take him back outside."

Looking at Ivy, Doc apologized. "Excuse me, Miss. I'm just an old fool with this old reindeer who almost squashed an overweight rabbit who has fallen in love with strawberries."

Taking hold of the doorknob, Doc hesitated. He stood there for a moment. Then, turning around with tears falling, he spoke.

"You still have those dimples, Ivy. Whenever you beat me at checkers, your dimples looked as if they were dancing. I can't believe you're here."

Walter was getting restless. Andy took him outside.

"I've thought of you, Doc, so many times."

As the snow kept falling, Ivy embraced her old friend.

"Oh, Doc," Ivy cried, not letting go. "I feel as if I've been on a long journey and finally made it home."

"You were always in my heart, sweet girl."

The wind was whistling about the barn as Andy returned, laughing.

"That Walter is stubborn. He thinks he belongs in here."

"That's my fault," said Doc, smiling. "I always let him in."

"That's why the animals love you."

"And that's why I have to move, Ivy."

"I saw the For Sale sign. Andy said you'd explain."

"It comes down to some neighbors who don't like living near my reindeer. It only took a few of them to complain for others to join in."

"When I lived next door, the neighbors loved having you here. You were always helping someone out."

"Back then I didn't have a barn full of reindeer."

"It's not just the neighbors, Ivy. It's the village," Andy added. "There are some new guys in charge. The original agreement Grampa made with the village concerning his putting up a building for the care of the reindeer within village limits has been nullified. We've gone back and forth with them, but there's no changing their narrow minds."

"What are you going to do, Doc?"

"The house has been sold. I have to be out by the end of February. I bought a place outside the village with a good-sized barn, but it needs some work, so I'm looking for a space to rent for the reindeer until the barn is ready."

"Will you keep your office here, Andy?"

"No. Everything on this property is included in the sale. I'm working with a Realtor."

"Enough talk about us. I've been keeping tabs on you, Ivy. Congratulations on your big award."

"Thanks, Doc. My scribbling on your front porch paid off. How did you hear about that?"

"It's a small community. Everybody knows one another. I've been friends with Vivian at the fabric shop for years. She's a talker, Ivy. Whenever I run into her, she fills me in on what's happening around here. We try to go for spaghetti at the diner on Sunday nights. We don't always make it. A few years ago, when we were ordering dessert, she happened to mention you being a successful designer in New York.

I told her I used to be your neighbor. Since then, she fills me in on anything she's heard about you. My guess is there's a lot of talking going on in that fabric shop."

"Yes, Vivian hears everything. I saw her earlier today. I didn't know she'd been hit by a car."

"Vivian's a strong gal. She's come a long way since then."

"Thank goodness she has her fabric shop. It gives her a reason to keep going."

"She's there most of the time now. Vivian thinks the world of you, Ivy. I heard about a gown you two worked on together."

"That gown was my first creation."

"Vivian's proud of that. She said you were a quick learner."

"That's because she was a wonderful instructor. It's nice you and Vivian go for spaghetti together."

"Like I said, we've known each other for years. She's good company." Hesitating, Doc added, "Always has been." Then he changed the subject. "Would you have time for a cup of coffee or tea?"

"I'd love a cup of coffee."

"How about you, Andy?"

"You and Ivy go ahead, Grampa. I have to check on Elena. Then I'll join you."

Walking along the lane, Ivy listened to her old friend. It was as if they'd never been apart.

"When I lost my son, the pain about crippled me. I don't know what I would have done if not for Andy. I never encouraged him to become a veterinarian. He came to me one day and told me that's what he wanted to do."

"I'm sure he watched you over the years. Only a person with a big heart can truly care for the animals. He inherited the gift of comforting from you."

"But it's a different time. I believe anyone who looks down on a reindeer is heartless. There's magic in the reindeer."

"Those types of people never believed in the first place, Doc." Stopping, Ivy looked over at what was now a yellow house. "When I look through those windows, I picture a family in turmoil, but there was love too. Now that I'm older, I realize my parents did the best they could."

"Do you keep in touch with Izzie? You were always protective of her."

"The last I knew she was married. For a while I'd call and leave messages. I'd never hear back, so after a while I gave up trying."

"You'll always be her older sister, Ivy. Just the other day I was thinking about the Christmas Eve when I put you two in the red cutter, and we went walking down the lane. A few minutes later, you jumped out and ran back the way we came."

"I had no choice. Izzie dropped a mitten and I needed to find it."

"I can still see you rushing back, holding the mitten, telling Izzie a little bird was sitting on it along the Mitten Path behind the barn. You explained how in the winter birds flew about the path looking for mittens to curl up on and stay warm. The mittens would be left by children in the neighborhood."

"I remember making that story up. I wanted Izzie to feel special. After all, it was Christmas Eve."

"You brought magic to Izzie's world. I'm certain she has not forgotten. A Mitten Path could have existed back then. Not anymore. The neighborhood has changed. The village has changed. I'm anxious to go."

"I'm glad you found a place you like, Doc."

"It's a great location for me but especially for the reindeer. Now we must find a location for Andy's office. The poor guy is dealing with a lot. Besides needing to relocate, he's having a problem with his daughter. Elena is going on eighteen. She's a senior in high school. Quite stunning, confused, and giving her father a hard time. His wife left when Elena took up with an older guy last year. Thankfully Elena came to her senses. I don't think she cared much about the guy. It was more about getting her parents' attention. One positive is Elena's love of animals. She and Walter are very close. Somehow, somewhere, Elena learned how to knit, so at certain times, Walter has what Elena calls 'reindeer decorations' hanging from his antlers. He doesn't mind. In fact, he seems quite proud. That old reindeer loves the pampering.

Elena is quite creative. She reminds me of you, Ivy. She's a good girl, just like you."

"Has Elena ever met Vivian?"

"Not that I'm aware. I know Vivian would have said something."

"Vivian is an ingenious lady as well as a wonderful listener."

"She's one in a million," replied Doc, holding the back door for Ivy. "Most of the reindeer I care for are old like me. I refuse to put them just anywhere only to have them wait to die. That's not living. Reindeer, like people, deserve to be treated with dignity. I know a woman who cares for reindeer at the end of their journey. She's an angel on earth as far as I'm concerned. She once told me even though her reindeer never flew around the world with Santa Claus, they've instilled wonder in so many children and deserve the dignity they've earned right up to their final breath in this world." Doc Armstrong added, with a sparkle in his eyes, "Remember that little reindeer you met in my barn on a Christmas Eve so many years ago? You and Izzie were convinced it was one of Santa's reindeer."

"We talked about that little reindeer all Christmas Day."

Once Doc had the coffee perking, he gave Ivy a quick tour. "I can't believe you've never been inside this house after all our games of checkers."

"Every time I told Mom that Izzie and I were coming over here to see you, she'd tell me not to stay too long because the animals needed you. And she said not to go in the house. You didn't have time to waste."

"I was never that busy. But it was nice of your mother to think so. Come with me, Ivy. I have something for you."

Going from a large, comfortable-looking living room with a beautiful bay window, then through a dining room, they ended up in a den lined with books still on shelves and a few odd items piled on an antique oak table.

"I've started going through boxes full of stuff saved over the years. Most of it is useless to anyone other than me, but there is one thing I want you to have."

Dusting off a box, Doc handed it to Ivy, explaining, "I'll never forget our times sitting on the front porch in the summertime."

"Oh, Doc, this game of checkers means so much to me. Thank you. Thank you!"

After a few tears, they were back in the kitchen enjoying their coffee. When Doc got up to cut a few slices of cranberry bread he'd made earlier, Andy walked through the door.

Elena was right behind him.

Chapter Seven

"WELL, ISN'T THIS A NICE SURPRISE," Doc said, smiling. "I've missed seeing you and so have the reindeer."

"I've missed you too, Gramps," replied Elena, quickly glancing at Ivy, moving her chestnut brown hair away from her face. "How's Walter?"

"He's busy as ever misbehaving, Elena. Still hanging out with Pearl."

Tall and slender with an ingenious style and green eyes, the young woman hugged her great-grandfather, adding, "I've been busy, too!"

"Schoolwork, I suppose."

"Let's not go there, Grampa."

Andy turned his attention to Ivy. "I'd like to introduce you to my daughter, Elena."

As Ivy stood, extending a hand, Andy continued, "Elena, meet Ivy. She grew up next door."

"It's very nice meeting you, Elena. I've heard you are a talented knitter, so much so that Walter has his own line of decorations."

Sitting next to her father, pulling a bottle of water out of her backpack, Elena replied, never taking her eyes off Ivy, "He doesn't have his antlers right now so I can't show you how handsome he looks with all of his decorations."

Elena paused, changing the subject. "I know who you are. I've been on your website. Why are you here, at Gramps kitchen table, eating bread and drinking coffee and talking about an old reindeer when you are a high-class designer? I don't get it."

"I told you, Elena. Ivy grew up next door."

"I know, Dad. But that was years ago. Why bother to come back here?"

"I haven't always been a designer with a studio on Madison Avenue, Elena. Growing up, I loved coloring and drawing and playing checkers with your great-grandfather. His support and encouragement helped me figure out why I loved doing those things. He became my best friend just when I needed one."

"He does the same with me. I pretend I'm not listening, but I am, Gramps."

Doc didn't say a word. Just winked at Elena.

"Three people made a difference in my life. Each of them bothered to care about an awkward, shy young girl. I came back to thank them, Elena. That's why I'm sitting at your great-grandfather's kitchen table. He is one of the three."

It was quiet in that old kitchen about to change hands until Elena spoke up.

"You're famous, Gramps."

"No. I'm not famous. I simply recognized a little girl with a need to be listened to and talents that needed to be nurtured."

It was turning dusk when the tooting of a horn, then brakes screeching, had everyone on their feet.

"It has to be Walter again!" yelled Doc, grabbing his flashlight.

"Oh no!" screamed Elena, as out the door and down the lane they ran.

The horn tooting continued. It was coming from a pickup. When seeing Doc, a door opened, and an unhappy guy jumped out.

"I just missed him again, Doc! That big old reindeer ran behind your barn. Next time I'll run him over! He needs to be put somewhere."

"Did you ever believe in Santa Claus?" Elena asked the man, standing in front of him, her arms crossed. "No. I don't think so. If you did, you wouldn't be talking about running down a reindeer, especially an old reindeer that brought Christmas magic to so many kids."

The guy didn't have time to reply. Elena went looking for Walter. Ivy and Andy followed.

"If something happened to Walter, Grampa and Elena would be devastated."

"When I lived here, cars and trucks were conscious of the homes situated along the lane."

"Like we told you earlier, so much has changed. I'm glad Grampa is moving. He doesn't deserve to be treated with such disrespect."

"How do you think he'll handle the move?"

"He'll be fine. The only problem is all those cubby-holes he has to go through. That will take him forever."

"I'd be happy to be here when he goes through them."

"That would be wonderful, Ivy. I must warn you; he'll have stories to tell about things he finds. If I'm there, I'll try to hurry him up."

"Please don't. I think when someone reaches a certain age, they've earned the right to tell their stories. Sometimes those stories are more like a history lesson on people and places that came before us. When someone has lived it, listening to them is invaluable."

"I never thought of his stories that way. There are times when he goes on and on and I tune him out. I'll start listening. Thanks for the insight, Ivy."

"You're welcome, Andy. I love how Elena spoke up to that guy driving his truck. What she said was the truth."

"Elena can be blunt, especially if she thinks she's right."

Andy changed his tone.

"Thanks for explaining to her why you are here. If something doesn't make sense to Elena, she'll seek the answer. When her mother and I divorced, she was like a lawyer. She still is at times."

"She's young, Andy. She's hurt. When my parents divorced, I turned angry. It got better, thanks to your grandfather. He helped me understand how some of that anger was hurt. Eventually I realized I still loved them. We could still be a family."

Elena was yelling. They found Walter. He was fine, back in his stall, eating hay.

The moon was out, leading Andy and Ivy inside the barn.

"Gramps had a wonderful idea, Dad."

"Your Gramps is full of ideas."

"This one is perfect, Andy. Since this will be my last Christmas in the big house, I'd like to go to the woods to get a Christmas tree. Bring hot chocolate. The decorations are already out. I was going to pack them, but I think they have one more Christmas left to hang on a Christmas tree in the bay window overlooking the lane."

"Could we go by sleigh, Gramps?"

"Sure can, young lady. I keep a few sleighs ready to go, and we'll have our choice of reindeer to take us to the woods."

Andy burst their bubble. "What woods?"

"Where we went before."

"We can't go there. The place has been sold. Trees are gone," Andy explained. "Maybe we can go to the convenience store on the corner. They always have lots of trees. We could still go in a sleigh. People would love that."

"I'd rather not get a tree if we have to go to a convenience store, Andy."

"I understand, Grampa. We'll figure it out in the morning. If we do go somewhere, would you like to come, Ivy?"

"I was thinking, Andy. I have a place just outside the village. It has some woods outback full of pine and spruce trees. You are welcome to come and look for the tree of your choice."

"How generous of you, Ivy."

"It's the least I can do, Doc."

"You could get a tree as well," Andy suggested.

"I won't be here long enough to enjoy it, but please, come find your Christmas tree. Talk about Christmas trees makes me think when I was little, and my mother thought I was sound asleep. But I was wide awake. I'd put my pillows at the end of my bed. Then I'd lie on my stomach, scoot down a bit, tuck my dolls and a few stuffed animals and favorite teddy bear around me, and stay very still as I looked out my window to get a view of your Christmas tree at nighttime. Sometimes the moon would be out above your house. Sometimes it would be snowing and blowing. Other times the snow would fall like precious little pearls. No matter what was going on outside, you always had the most beautiful Christmas tree inside."

"Gramps's trees are always perfect," said Elena.

"I'm sure we'll find another perfect one tomorrow. If you come around ten thirty, we can head out to the woods, find the tree, and then go back for something to eat."

"You cook, too?"

"Not very often, Andy. Have a hearty breakfast before you come."

"I'll say good night, Ivy. I must feed the crew out in the barn and get them to bed."

"I'll help you, Gramps. I can tell Walter needs me."

"You made those two very happy, Ivy. They had their hearts set on one last Christmas tree," remarked Andy, walking alongside Ivy up the lane.

"I think it's a good idea. It will be like celebrating all the Christmases that took place in that house throughout the years."

With the moon going in and out of rolling clouds and snowflakes falling, Ivy continued as they approached the yellow house with a yellow fence.

"I loved living here. We had a big yard with a flower garden. My bedroom was my favorite place. It was right up there, in the back, away from my sister, with stairs going down to the kitchen. My closet was a good size. Most of my stuffed animals were in there, lined up in doll beds. One of the floorboards was loose, so I turned it into a secret spot. That's where I kept my diary and some of my first, what I called, designs. I put a doll bed over it so not even Izzie knew about it. I squeezed my pine desk in there too. My grandfather made it for me. It was my first desk. It remains my favorite desk."

A car turning onto the lane interrupted Ivy, but only for a moment.

"My mother told us we'd be moving, but she didn't say when. She did tell me one Saturday morning as I was going out the door to play checkers with Doc that it'd be the last time I'd be doing that so I should tell him I was moving. Telling Doc was gut-wrenching. When Izzie and I got home from school one day the following week, she told us to get in the car. We thought we were going on an adventure because some of our favorite things were in the backseat. Boy, we were surprised a little while later when she parked in front of a tall building, explaining it was our new home."

"The apartment is on the third floor," she told us. "You have to share a bedroom."

Izzie started crying. She wanted her favorite dolls.

"They are in your room," she told Izzie. "On your bed."

"I never asked about my desk or diary or designs. I was afraid of the answer."

Looking up at her old bedroom window, Ivy admitted she'd never told anyone about the day they moved away. "I thought I was beyond all of that. Now, standing by the house, it feels like yesterday."

"You told me something was pulling you back here, but you couldn't put your finger on it. Maybe it was loose ends."

"Loose ends?"

"Unfinished business. You never got to say goodbye to this place that was your home, with a bedroom you obviously cherished. That closet was your safe space holding your most treasured possessions. There was never any closure. To some, it wouldn't matter. But to you, Ivy, being so connected to your surroundings, with a creativeness that was taking shape even back then, it mattered. It still does. Here you are an adult, looking through the eyes of a child who never got to say goodbye."

With the snow still flitting about, Ivy kept looking up at that bedroom window.

"You're right, Andy. There are loose ends that need closure. Being taken away from here left feelings of emptiness inside me that no award or accolade could fill. That emptiness brought me back home."

"Makes me think of Grampa wanting one more Christmas, one more Christmas tree to decorate and put on display in front of the bay window. That is closure for him."

A lamppost by the back porch of the yellow house came on. Before

Ivy could react, the door opened, and someone peered out at the two standing there in the snow.

"Is that you, Andy?"

"Yes. I hope we didn't wake you, Tom."

"Not at all. Something going on?"

"Everything's fine. This is Ivy. She used to live here when she was a young girl."

"It's a pleasure meeting you, Ivy."

"Nice meeting you, Tom."

"Ivy was telling me how much she loved the house."

"My wife and I have been here about ten years now. It's a great place to raise our two little ones. Lots of space. A big yard and we love having reindeer next door."

A woman with her hair pulled back in a ponytail joined Tom. "This is Ivy, honey. She grew up here. Our home was her family's home."

"It's a pleasure to meet you, Ivy. I'm Carrie."

"So very nice to meet you, Carrie."

"We love living here. The people we bought it from did some renovating. We've done a little painting, but once the twins were born, we put any renovating ideas we had on hold."

Pausing, Carrie added, "You're more than welcome to come in. The boys are still up, so please excuse the mess."

"You don't mind?"

"I went back home this summer to visit my mom. We got talking about the place we lived in when I was growing up. A few hours later, we drove by it and the owner was out front cutting the grass. I pulled up to the curb. One thing led to another, and he invited us inside the house. I learned nothing stays the same, so I don't mind at all, Ivy. I understand."

A few seconds later, Ivy was going up steps she used to run down. Andy was right behind her.

Chapter Eight

DESPITE THE YEARS PASSING BY, Ivy was certain she could smell banana bread baking in the oven as she walked onto the sunporch where she and Izzie would play, even in the wintertime. Her mother most always made the banana bread on her days off. It was Ivy's grandmother's recipe. They all loved it, especially warm with butter.

Going into the kitchen, Ivy noted the room was wide open. Gone was the countertop where she and her sister stood on chairs, helping their mother roll out cookie dough. Then, taking cookie cutters from a cupboard drawer, they'd cut out all kinds of shapes to make the best sugar cookies ever. The white enamel cupboards where those cookie cutters were kept were gone, as was the clock ticking over the cellar door. The walls were now mustard yellow. The floor was wood. The windows were new and dressed in blinds.

"We spend a lot of time in here," Carrie explained, leading them past the backstairs. Ivy took a quick glance, but the lights were off up in her old bedroom.

"Was this your dining room, Ivy? The previous owners ran a business, and this room was their home office. The first thing Carrie and I did was make this room the dining room."

"It was ours as well," said Ivy, remembering Christmas Eve suppers when her mother made a special dinner, including rice pudding, the

family's favorite banana bread, and her hot fudge sauce served over vanilla ice cream. The house would be full of relatives.

Pointing out a smaller room that used to be lined with bookshelves,
Tom explained it was now a toy room. "That's where the noise is coming from. The boys are all wound up with Christmas getting closer."

Tom called out to them.

"Charlie and Bobby, come here for a minute."

The twins came running. Both had light-brown curly hair and
freckles.

"I want you to meet Ivy. She grew up in this house."

"I'm happy to meet the two of you. Sounds like you were having
fun in there."

"We're building a giant tower," said Bobby.

"Did Santa Claus leave you presents here?" Charlie asked.

"He certainly did."

"Did you see his reindeer?"

"I did one year, Charlie," Ivy replied, remembering that Christmas
Eve spent with Doc and Izzie.

Seconds later the noise continued in the toy room as Carrie led the
way into the double living room. It looked unchanged to Ivy.

"Even with the Christmas tree in the corner, there's still plenty of
room," said Tom.

"That's the same corner where my father put our tree every year,"
remarked Ivy, thinking the trees they had were so much bigger. As they
started up the stairs, Ivy noted the floor register in a small hallway connecting to the dining room. She was certain it was the same one she
and Izzie would jump over until they were told to stop.

The bathroom had been enlarged and remodeled.

There were still four bedrooms. The twins had Izzie's old room.
Pink walls had turned blue. Polka dot curtains were now puppy dogs.
Bunk beds were along the opposite wall to where Izzie had her single
bed with lots of pillows and stuffed animals on top.

The back bedroom was the last room left to visit.

"Tom and I decided this would be our room because of the pri-
vacy," Carrie explained. "Watch it. There are three short steps down."

Ivy almost corrected her until she realized there were three steps instead of the two when it had been her bedroom.

"The previous owners had one child, a daughter, and this was her bedroom. They told me they didn't hold back with the renovations."

"I don't recognize it," Ivy replied, noticing her closet was gone. In its place sat an oversized dresser with a large mirror. From that point on, Ivy considered the tour to be over.

A few minutes later, she and Andy were walking up the lane.

"That's one loose end tied up. It proves you can't go back."

"You'll always have the memories as you keep moving forward."

"That's for sure. Even though the closet was gone, I could still see it there, along with everything I left inside it before going to school on my last morning in that house."

"Are you hungry, Ivy? It must be going on six o'clock. We could go to the diner not far from here."

"I'd love to, Andy. I worked there on weekends when I was in high school."

"I think it's the same owners. They'll be thrilled to meet a former weekend employee turned famous designer."

"You're too kind, Andy. Get in. I'll drive," said Ivy, moving the checkers game she'd put on the passenger's seat to the back.

"Let's stop at the barn so I can ask Elena and Grampa to join us."

By half past six the four of them were on their way.

"I love that you drive a truck, Ivy. I wish my friends could see me riding in the back seat of designer Ivy Nolan's truck. They'd be so jealous!"

"I know Walter was jealous," laughed Doc. "He wanted to join us. I told him maybe next time."

The snow had let up.

For a weeknight, the diner was busy. They were told to seat themselves, so Ivy led the way to a booth near the back.

"The booths haven't changed."

Looking around, Ivy added, "I don't think anything has changed."

"As long as the food is good, that's what matters."

"I never had one complaint when I waited table here, Andy."

"You worked here?"

"I did, Elena, during my junior and senior year. I liked it, and the tips were good."

"You worked here? What's your name? The owner likes to see her employees return for a meal," asked their waitress, who had a beehive and layers of eye makeup.

"Ivy Nolan."

"Is that your married name?"

"I'm not married."

"She's not married, but she is famous," added Elena, filling the waitress in.

By the look on her face, the woman was clueless. Handing out the menus, the waitress told them she'd be back for their orders.

It turned out everything was delicious. When the waitress brought their desserts, an older woman followed with a pot of coffee.

"Mrs. Costa, it's so nice to see you!"

"When I heard you were here, Ivy, I had to come in and say hello and bring your table a pot of our delicious coffee on the house."

"That is so nice of you. The place is busy as ever."

"We've been fortunate over the years. I hear you've been quite successful. I'm not surprised, Ivy."

"Thank you. Your diner was my first job. I enjoyed working for you."

A woman walking by with three children stopped in front of the table.

"It is you! I heard your name. I can't believe it, Ivy. Remember me? We went to school together. I was Angie Wilson. I'm Angie Hayward now. This is Janet, Sue, and Zachary. I saw you on Ellen after you received your big award. Congratulations!"

Ivy tried to keep it brief. It was getting busier, and others walking by slowed down to get a look at the designer. An older man, with his coat still zipped, stopped, and with one cruel remark aimed at Doc, put a damper on the moment.

"I see those reindeer of yours are still on the lane. Time is running out. This is not the North Pole. Understand?"

The man didn't wait for Doc to reply. He disappeared.

Andy was on his feet. "I'll find that loser, Grampa."

"No, Andy. He'd like it if you made a scene. That would give him even more of an excuse to go after the reindeer. Let's leave quietly. No sense in stirring up more trouble."

"I know who that was, Gramps. I go to school with his grand-daughter. She's obnoxious, too."

"Let it go, Elena. We must think of the reindeer. Keeping them safe is top priority."

The ride back to the barn was subdued until Ivy reminded them, they'd be getting a Christmas tree the next day.

"We'll have a fun time. I can't promise a meal like we just had."

"Well, that's a good thing, Ivy," Doc remarked.

They laughed the rest of the way. Ivy could tell he was anxious to check the reindeer. The minute she pulled up next to the barn, he hurried out of the truck, talking as he went along. Everyone followed.

"What a pleasure to have you back home, Ivy. Don't be worrying about Walter and friends. We'll find them a safe place real soon."

"I've missed you, Doc. I asked Andy what I could do to help you get ready to move, and he suggested I be here when you go through your cubbyholes. I wouldn't be telling you what to do with your stuff. I'd be here to support you."

"I'd like that, Ivy. We'll talk more. Now get home. And drive carefully. Deer are everywhere!"

Saying good night, Andy handed Ivy his business card. "I wrote my private cell number on the back."

"Good idea."

Ivy reached in her purse for a business card. "Here's my number if you need to reach me."

"Thanks. I enjoyed your company, Ivy."

"I had a wonderful time, Andy. I'm glad you were with me when I went on my house tour. It gave me a lot to think about."

"I'm glad I could be there for you."

"Think Doc will be okay after being verbally attacked?"

"Grampa is tough. But that man in the diner is one of many and even more reason why we must get the reindeer settled. I wouldn't put anything past them."

"I don't understand their anger toward Doc and his reindeer."

"We are living in strange times, but it only makes us stronger."

"You sound like your grandfather."

"I take that as a compliment, considering he about raised me."

"Wait, Ivy. Don't leave." It was Elena hurrying out of the barn.

"Pearl wants to say good night, and so do I."

The sight of Elena running toward her, hugging a rabbit in the moonlight, reminded Ivy of that Christmas Eve walk down the lane. There's a lot to be said about the magic of snow falling gently to the earth.

After saying good night, Ivy was on her way. Doc was right. Deer were everywhere.

The caretaker had plowed the driveway. He even shoveled both front and back steps and put a package by the door. Fifteen minutes after getting home, Ivy had changed into something warm and comfortable and was making a cup of ginger tea.

Before sitting at the kitchen table to enjoy it, Ivy took a closer look at the package. It was from Lawrence. Seeing his penmanship made Ivy realize how much she missed him. They were always together. She'd encourage him to take vacations, but the farthest he ever went was his parents' restaurant. Opening the box, pulling back layers of tissue paper, crumpled newspaper, and foil, Ivy realized he'd been at the restaurant again after she found beautifully packaged gifts of tiramisu.

A note was included:

Layers and layers of love sent your way, from my parents—and me.
Lawrence

The simple note in a box full of tiramisu added to the emotions of the last few days. Ivy realized Lawrence had taken care of tomorrow's dessert without even knowing it. *He's always taking care of me,* Ivy thought as she picked up her cup of tea and went over to the window facing the back fields glistening under the moonlight. Standing there, she noticed deer running along a hedgerow behind the barn. Looking at the structure as more deer came running, Ivy moved closer to the window. A thought was taking shape. *Of course*, she told herself, hurrying over to the table.

Seconds later she had Andy on the phone.

"Ivy, is there something wrong?"

"I think I've tied another loose end."

"Two in one day. That's wonderful."

"Andy. I found a place for the reindeer."

"What? Where are you?"

"I'm home. I'm talking about my barn. I never use it, Andy. It's in perfect condition. It's the perfect solution. I don't know why I didn't think of it sooner. Take a look at it tomorrow, and if you think it will work, we'll talk to Doc."

"Are you sure, Ivy? It means we'll be in and out of your barn when you're not there."

"I realize that, but if I can help Doc in any way, I will."

"That is generous of you, Ivy. I won't say a thing until you and I talk it over. What would you like me to bring?"

"Your reindeer. Good night, Andy." Exhausted, Ivy turned the lights out and went upstairs to bed.

Around two o'clock in the morning, the wind started howling, waking Ivy out of a sound sleep. Pulling the blankets around her, Ivy began thinking about the cooking she'd soon be undertaking. She ended up calling Lawrence. Ivy knew he wouldn't mind. Whether creating a new dress or an entire line, Ivy would call him, no matter the time, to mull over various designs and fabrics.

Lawrence answered on the second ring. After thanking him for the tiramisu, Ivy asked for his assistance in figuring out her menu.

"You know I don't enjoy cooking. This must be simple. I don't have hours to prepare enough to feed five people."

"Five is easy. I'll email you some suggestions. Whatever you choose, include some fresh Italian bread and a tossed salad on your menu. They help to satisfy anyone's hunger."

"Thank you again for dessert. By the way, we're going searching for a Christmas tree in the back woods later today. A real Christmas tree, Lawrence, with branches you don't snap into place."

"Are you getting a tree?"

"I'd love to, but no. I won't be here long enough to enjoy it. The tree is for my friend, Doc."

"From what you've told me, Ivy, you're having a wonderful time back home. That makes me happy."

After talking a little business, they said good night.

Before getting back into bed, Ivy wrote herself a note to call Vivian first thing in the morning. Ivy's plan was to invite her for the late lunch. Hopefully Vivian would be that fifth person around the table.

Despite being tired, Ivy kept watch of the snowflakes passing by her window.

She was soon sound asleep.

Chapter Nine

A LITTLE BEFORE FIVE, Ivy was showered, dressed, and in the kitchen with recipes printed out and the coffee perking. Ivy was again thankful for the caretaker. She called him in need of a few ingredients, and he delivered them before she had her second cup of coffee.

Knowing Vivian was an early riser, Ivy called and invited her before seven. She hesitated at first. When Ivy told her she'd have a taxi pick her up and bring her home, Vivian accepted.

Choosing a pasta casserole that sounded soothing on a snowy day plus a side vegetable dish, Ivy went to work. She added her grandmother's rice pudding with raisins to the menu as well as her banana bread with cinnamon swirls. They were the only recipes Ivy knew by heart. To her surprise, she got into a groove, mixing and stirring until her phone rang a little before eight.

"Good morning, Andy. I hope you are hungry."

"I skipped my toast. I want to have enough room to enjoy your hard work."

"So far, so good. How's everything there?"

Andy explained he was just checking in. Then he went on about Elena. "I told her she could take today off from school to come with me, and this morning her mother told her just the opposite."

"What did Elena do?"

"She stormed out and came to my place. Her mother and I just got into it over the phone after I told her about our plans for the day."

"What did you tell her?"

"I told her about you. I explained Elena had the opportunity to spend more time with you today, but she still wouldn't give an inch. I made the argument that spending time with a highly successful designer who grew up next to my grandfather could influence Elena more than reading about some highly successful person on the web or in a book."

"I can't comment, Andy. It's between the three of you. But I will say this. When I was Elena's age, working a weekend shift at the diner, I met a woman who was somehow related to the cook. She'd stopped to touch base with him on her way back to New York City. I remember her first name was Paulette. Turns out she was a successful model and movie star, born right down the road from where I am now. I studied her makeup. I wanted my eyes to look just like hers and to wear red lipstick like she did. But what really caught my attention was what she was wearing. Rather, it was the material it was made out of and the way it was sewn to create a style all its own. I'd never seen anything like it. It piqued my interest even more than the makeup. My point is, meeting that successful woman at the diner was a pivotal moment for me at an impressionable age. Up until then I'd never met anyone from beyond the county line."

"I understand what you are saying, Ivy. That's the point I tried making to Elena's mother."

By the time ten thirty came around, Ivy had the table set, her clothes changed, makeup on, hair brushed, and she only connected with Lawrence a few times for help. With it getting dark by a little after four, she wanted to give them enough time to find a Christmas tree.

Vivian arrived a little early. She was all dressed up and smiling like she used to smile.

After helping her out of the cab, Ivy embraced her friend. "You look lovely, Vivian. I'm so glad you came."

"Thank you, my dear Ivy, for inviting me. I haven't been anywhere but the shop in ages."

After speaking to the cab driver, Ivy walked alongside Vivian up the shoveled pathway and inside her home.

"Oh, my! How charming. Your creativeness is everywhere."

"Thanks, Vivian. Please, come in and get comfortable."

"That won't be hard to do. Something smells delicious, Ivy. I didn't realize you could cook."

"Lawrence helped me."

"Is that young man here?"

"No. I kept calling him and he kept saving me."

"I won't say a word."

"You might when you have dessert." Ivy went on to explain about his beautifully packaged gifts of tiramisu. With everything ready, they sat down by the fireplace while waiting for the others.

"I hope you didn't mind my asking Doc and his grandson and great-granddaughter to join us."

"Not at all. Doc and I go way back. If I've ever needed anything, he's always been there for me."

"Doc told me about you two going out most Sunday evenings to the diner for their spaghetti dinner special. I could tell he looks forward to going with you."

"I look forward to our Sunday evenings as well."

"I remember how much I enjoyed working with you creating that velvet dress. Sometimes you didn't have to say a word. Your eyes did the speaking, Vivian."

"If I'm into something, words escape me."

"When Doc congratulated me on my award, he explained you told him and went on to say you're the best of friends."

Ivy paused, clearing her throat. "But, his eyes, Vivian, said so much more. Is there more? I'm asking because I care about you two."

Vivian didn't hold back. It was as if she'd been waiting for someone to knock down a wall built up over the years.

"Your perception is as keen as your sense of design, Ivy. I've never discussed Doc with anyone."

As logs shifted and crackled in the fireplace, Vivian told her story. "I fell in love right out of high school with a man who was ten years older than me and quite possessive. Eventually he told me what to wear, so I wouldn't attract another man. I wasn't allowed to put makeup on, and Ivy, you know I love my makeup. It got to the point I couldn't leave the apartment without him.

"It all came to a head on a Saturday evening. I was sick with the flu. We didn't have anything to take for a headache, so after he passed out from drinking, I hurried to the store. When I returned, he was waiting for me. Grabbed me the minute I walked through the door and beat me up. Then he used his belt to finish the job. I don't remember passing out, but when I woke up, I was in the hospital. I later learned a woman I'd met in the building heard me screaming and called the police. Long story short, I never saw him again. That same woman later told me he took off with some girl he was seeing behind my back."

"Oh, Vivian. You are even stronger than I realized.

"I was too embarrassed to go back home, so I called a cousin who lived here. She was so kind to me. She knew of some places that were hiring. One was the fabric shop. I didn't know a thing about sewing, but all those bolts of fabric intrigued me. I was hired part time, but it wasn't long before I was full time. There used to be a soda fountain around the corner. I'd go there on payday day for lunch. That's where I met Doc. That day the place was crowded. All the tables were taken. I decided to leave and come back later, but a handsome man with a pleasant smile asked if I'd like to sit with him. Oh, Ivy, I was so hesitant. I swore I'd never have anything to do with a man again, but there was something about him. When he complimented me on my dress, I almost cried."

Clearing her throat, Vivian continued. "I saw him again a few weeks later when my cousin left me in charge of her cat. The poor thing got hit by a car. I panicked. I looked in the yellow pages for a veterinarian. One ad emphasized, 'No appointment necessary.' I called a cab, and when I walked in the doctor's office, there he was, Ivy. He remembered me from the soda fountain."

"So, what then? I feel like I should be serving popcorn."

"The cat was only bruised, but Doc felt it should stay the night, explaining a doctor would be there and, if there was a problem, he'd get a call. Doc went on to say he was about to leave and asked if I'd like to go for a drink. I was a wreck. But he was such a gentleman. We ended up at a quiet place not far from his office. It was a summer evening. We sat in a corner and talked. Real talk, not just pleasantries. When he told me there was sadness in my eyes, I began crying, and out came all that horrible stuff, including the beating. He told me any man who did that to a woman was a monster. He said more than once, I deserved better. Someone played a slow song on the jukebox, and Doc asked me to dance. Wrapped in his arms, I finally felt safe. Felt at peace. I fell in love instantly. All the vows I'd made about never this and never that went flying out the door. I spent the night with him, Ivy, and the next night after that. We couldn't get enough of each other. But then one night, it was over."

Vivian stopped and asked for a drink of water.

"I could tell you cared for each other," said Ivy. "But I never realized it was such a love story. Why did it end? It's obvious you still love each other."

"Doc enlisted in the army. It was during the Vietnam War and he felt a sense of duty. On top of that, he'd been engaged but called it off. That's when we met. Turned out his fiancée was pregnant. Her family came down hard on him. Being the sweet man that he is, he felt obligated. So, Doc married her and went off to war. I'd never been as sad as I was the night we said goodbye. For the longest time, I felt dead inside. Doc was my one true love, and I lost him."

"But you didn't."

"No, I didn't. He began writing me. I was so afraid something was going to happen to him that I'd write back despite his being married. My letters kept getting more personal, and it wasn't long before I was telling him how much I loved him. He would always tell me I was the love of his life. At some point, I realized I needed something to sink my teeth into. I had no clue what that was until my boss decided to sell her shop. With her support, I bought the business. I threw myself into it. I did special orders. Went to New York to buy fabric. Held fashion shows, and all along, I kept Doc tucked away in my heart."

"What happened when he came back?"

"By then, his son had been born. He bought the place on the lane because of the barn behind it."

"Was he happy?"

"Doc kept my letters. He brought them home only to have his wife find them. She threatened to take their son and leave and make sure Doc never saw his boy again. He stayed with her for the sake of their son, who was killed in a car accident years later. Doc told me he couldn't leave her after they'd lost him. It nearly killed her."

"I understand, but she has since passed away. You and Doc could be married."

"By then we had our own lives."

"Have you talked about marriage?"

"No. I feel it is not my place to bring that up. We know we love each other. Even at our age, we feel it with every touch. A lot of married people can't say that. I am blessed and so very much in love."

"What a movie your story would make, Vivian."

"You have an interesting story as well, Ivy. We are very much alike. Both of us enjoy creating with fabric. We're both in love."

"While I am not in love, I do have a story to tell you."

Ivy went on about the night of the Holiday Ball at the downtown Grand Hotel.

"John had reserved us a room. He told me more than once it included free champagne. When we were dressed and ready to go downstairs, he tried to unzip my gown and get me into bed."

"I have to ask. Did he like your beautiful velvet gown?"

"All he wanted to do was get it off me."

"Did he?"

"No. I told him we should go dancing and let the anticipation build. That way it would be more fun later."

"You're quick on your feet. I never would have thought to say that when a guy wanted me in bed."

"Well, it didn't work."

"What happened?"

"Just before the last dance he told me he wouldn't be seeing me again, so I should hurry upstairs and jump in bed with him."

"What?"

"He told me he was going home for Christmas break and not coming back because he was getting married."

"And I've thought all along you had a wonderful time. What did you do?"

"I told him to get his things, pay for the room, and get out of my sight. Then I ran upstairs, threw myself on the bed, and cried myself to sleep. I woke up around two in the morning—and Vivian, please don't get mad at me—but I took my beautiful custom-designed green velvet gown off and threw it in the trash. Then I tossed whatever else I had hanging around into my suitcase and left."

"I probably would have done the same thing."

"I know, but it was the first gown I designed. It meant more to me than just being a gown. It represented our hard work together and our friendship that came from it."

"Put it into perspective. It was just a gown. What happened after you left? Where did you go?"

Ivy told Vivian about sitting on the swing outside in the cold and the snow and how Murphy came out and saved her.

"He is a sweetheart. Murphy would always be helping the community. I am not surprised he came to your rescue."

Ivy was about to go on about the hot chocolate but stopped when she heard what sounded like bells ringing outside. Looking out a window, she began laughing.

"Oh, Vivian. They came in a sleigh pulled by reindeer with a cargo sled attached behind. The way the wind's blowing, Doc's beard makes him look like Santa Claus."

"As far as I'm concerned, he is."

Chapter Ten

THE FARMHOUSE WAS FULL OF HOLIDAY spirit, especially when Doc spotted Vivian sitting by the fireplace.

"What a wonderful surprise," he roared, giving her a hug.

"Aren't you the silly one," Vivian replied, her face flushed. "Ivy told me you came by sleigh."

"The snow is perfect for a sleigh ride. We'll come back tomorrow with the truck to pick up the tree."

Turning to Ivy, Doc continued. "Judging from the aromas, I have to say you're a top designer and a fine cook as well."

"That's generous of you, Doc, but I had a helper who gets most of the credit."

"Where is your helper?"

"Lawrence and I were connected online. He's my assistant. I'd be nothing without him."

"Is he a designer, too?" Elena asked.

"He could be, but he prefers the business side. I met him at the Fashion Institute."

"Where's that?"

"In New York."

"I've never been there."

"I never went to the city until I attended the school. If it hadn't been for those three special people, I probably would have stayed here for the rest of my life."

Moving closer to Vivian, Ivy introduced her to Elena.

"So very nice to meet you, Elena. You have your father's smile."

"Thanks, Vivian. I try to tell Elena we could be twins, but she doesn't agree," said Andy, helping himself to some hors d'oeuvres sitting atop a plank pine table decorated with small pine branches arranged in an antique crock.

"I look like me," Elena declared. "Not my father. Not my mother."

Vivian changed the subject. "Ivy tells me you enjoy knitting."

"I do, especially for Walter."

"Did you bring Walter today, Doc?"

"No, Vivi. Walter's slowing down."

"Aren't we all?" Vivian laughed, turning her attention back to Elena.

"Anytime you'd like to stop by my fabric shop, I'd love to show you around. I always say to those who don't sew, if you can knit, you can sew."

Ivy told Elena about her first visit to Vivian's shop.

"With all that fabric, it was like being in a candy store. I couldn't sew, but once I was in her shop, I wanted to. Thanks to Vivian, I learned how."

"I don't know what I want to do."

"I'm not saying you have to become a seamstress, Elena. Just pointing out how being surrounded by all that fabric allowed my creativity to kick in."

"If you can knit for a reindeer, you are creative, Elena," added Vivian.

"Are you at your shop every day?"

"I'm married to the place, Elena" replied Vivian, glancing over at Doc. "Stop by. If you ever want to earn some money, I'm always in need of someone to straighten the shelves. Most days the bolts of fabric are a mess."

After Ivy walked around serving hot apple cider punch in stoneware mugs to her guests, she went into the kitchen to check on things before heading to the woods. Andy followed.

"Need any help, Ivy?"

"Thanks, Andy, but I think we are good to go."

"Being in the kitchen with you is a nice feeling. You have a lovely home."

"That's kind of you to say."

"I've always liked this property. There's something peaceful about it."

From out of the north came a slight breeze, moving the wind chimes hanging near the back porch.

"I love hearing the wind chimes and the trains in the distance and the geese coming across the river. Things I considered to be nothing when I lived at home mean so much to me now."

"Do you think I could ever mean something to you, Ivy?"

Holding on to the rice pudding even tighter as she took it out of the oven, Ivy set it on the counter. While getting a serving spoon from a drawer, she replied, "I've been so absorbed in creating a brand that something had to give, and that turned out to be a relationship. I have nothing left to devote to anyone."

"What about Lawrence?"

"My Lawrence?"

"Yes."

"He is my friend." With that, Ivy covered the rice pudding for later.

"I'm sorry, Ivy. I spoke out of turn."

"No problem, Andy. Here's the key to the barn. We can show it to Doc later, if you think he'd be interested. If so, I do not want one cent from him."

"I understand. I'll be right back."

As he opened the door, Ivy called out to him.

"Andy?"

"Yes, Ivy?"

"I think you're quite charming.

Chapter Eleven

As the mantle clock in the dining room announced the twelve o'clock hour, everyone was bundling up. Ivy was coming down the stairs with blankets just as Andy was coming in from the kitchen. They took a minute to talk.

"It's perfect, Ivy. All we have to do is move the reindeer in and get them comfortable. Work is scheduled to begin on Grampa's new barn in early March. If there are no surprises, we'd hope to move the reindeer in around the end of May."

"Wonderful. Now let's go find Doc a Christmas tree."

No one could get Vivian to stay behind. With Andy on one side of her and Doc on the other, she made it into the back of the sleigh, between Ivy and Elena.

"Cover up, everyone. It's going to get cold. Once we are in the woods, we'll be protected. Hot chocolate is in a thermos underneath my seat. Cups included."

"You came prepared, Doc."

"When little ones think you're Santa Claus, you have to be ready for anything, Ivy, especially when going after a Christmas tree."

Doc alerted the reindeer. It was time to go. In seconds their hoofs were breaking through the drifts as the December sun sifted through falling snowflakes. No one spoke. The business of Christmas was at hand. Doc still had his skill of maneuvering a sleigh dragging a cargo sled and pulled by reindeer about trees and hedgerows. While he'd never been in those woods, it didn't matter. He brought them to a stop in a most peaceful clearing.

"Ivy, you have yourself a little bit of heaven back here. The silence is comforting."

"I hope to get out here more than I have, especially this time of year."

"What sort of a tree are we after, Gramps?"

"Doesn't matter as long as it's full and reaches the ceiling, Elena."

"I'll stay here while the rest of you find the tree."

Doc wrapped an extra blanket around Vivian, whispering, "Stay warm, my love."

"Let's split up. Andy, you and I can head beyond those birch trees. Elena and Ivy, you head toward those scotch pines. Don't wander too far. It looks mighty dense in places."

"We won't be far, Doc."

"Remember, Ivy, a tree is always bigger than it looks out in the woods."

Once on their own, Elena wondered why they were bothering to go to the woods for a Christmas tree. "I mean, why bother when they're for sale all over the place?"

"It's more about being in the woods. There's so much to see."

"Look around, Ivy! It's all just trees."

"But there's so much more."

"Like what?"

"Like these beautiful bushes," Ivy pointed out. "Look underneath. They're not so beautiful. Be careful of the thorns. And look over there. See those precious little snow buntings? They are my favorite winter bird. These tree branches in front of us are full of little pinecones. We used to collect pinecones and make decorations out of them. And those tracks in the snow? They are rabbit tracks."

"How do you know so much?"

"Before my parents divorced, we'd go to the woods for our Christmas tree. My mother insisted it had to be a huge tree. My father spent what seemed like hours putting it in the corner of our double living room. That's when we lived next door to Doc. After my father had the lights strung, my sister and I helped our mother decorate it. Most times that took all day. When we finished, we'd sit in front of the tree with it all lit up. My father collected old record albums. He even had a record player that was his father's. So, as we sat looking at the tree, he'd play his favorite Christmas album over and over again just so he could hear 'Silent Night.' It was his favorite song anytime of the year. Mom served her special Christmas punch with sliced strawberries and sugar cookies we'd made the day before. It was a special time."

Ivy paused. Watching the snow buntings, she added, "I can still see my parents sitting together on the sofa."

"What happened after they divorced? Did you still go to the woods for a tree?"

"No. After my father left, my mother sold the house and the three of us moved into a small apartment. I was so angry at her. I missed my room, our yard, my father, Doc, and his animals. I placed all the blame on my mother. I never invited any of my friends to the apartment. Actually, I didn't have any friends."

"My parents are divorced," Elena said, checking out pinecones on low-hanging branches.

Ivy stayed silent.

Elena kept talking. "It's my mother's fault. She's still mean to my father. Occasionally during the night, I hear her crying, so I turn my TV on."

"When I'd hear my mother yell at my father over the phone, I'd get even angrier at her," Ivy explained.

"So, if your parents were divorced, you lived in a small apartment, and you had no friends, how did you get to be a famous designer?" Elena asked as she took pictures of snow buntings with her phone.

"While I didn't have friends, again, I did have those three adults who were there for me. Doc was the most influential. I didn't realize just how much until I was in my second year at the Institute and ended up in the hospital with food poisoning. Scared, I called my father. I could tell he'd been drinking. He laughed off the food poisoning, telling me to watch what I eat. He hung up a few minutes later. Then I called my mother. Being a nurse, she had questions for my nurse. Later that night, I heard my door open. It was my mother. She drove all the way to be with me and stayed until I was released. That's when I realized what Doc had been telling me for the longest time."

"What?"

"In my eyes, my father could do no wrong. I blamed my mother for ending, what I considered to be, my perfect life. Doc would often tell me in his gentle way to be kind to my mother; tell me I wasn't in my mother's shoes, meaning I didn't know what it was like to be married to my father."

Ivy and Elena kept walking as snow quietly fell about the trees. Ivy spotted a spruce that was a possibility, but when they got closer, they saw it wasn't as big as it needed to be.

"Back then," Ivy continued, "I was unaware of how hard my mother tried to keep us all together. My father was liked by lots of people. Most didn't know he was a quiet drinker. He stayed home to do his drinking. You see, Elena, throughout all those years, Doc was telling me to be kind to my mother because he realized she was the stronger one in their relationship. My mother needed my support, but I never gave her an inch. When I think about it, she was there for me as much as she could be."

"Did you stop seeing your father?"

"No, and that was because of Vivian."

Ivy shared her experience of meeting John and his invitation to the Holiday Ball at the downtown Grand Hotel.

"It was a dressy affair. Because I wanted my gown to be original, I needed fabric and a seamstress, and somehow, I needed to design the gown. I'd walked by Vivian's shop a few times, so I knew where to go for fabric. It turned out Vivian helped me with so much more. Over time we had some good talks. Because of those talks, I was able to understand how some people, like my father, are ill-equipped to deal with their problems. That didn't make my father a bad person. I knew he loved me in his own way. Vivian encouraged me to concentrate on myself. She told me I had a unique eye for design after I sketched what turned out to be my gown. Working with Vivian inspired me. That was all I needed."

"How was that Holiday Ball? What was your dress like? How cute was your date?"

Elena kept asking questions as she noted some rabbit tracks disappearing into a hedgerow. Ivy answered them all, going on to explain what a disaster the evening turned out to be.

"That guy was a jerk."

"Yes, he was a total jerk, but because of him I met another wonderful adult."

Ivy talked about Murphy.

"After he persuaded me to go back inside and have a cup of hot chocolate with him, he stayed. It was two o'clock in the morning and he stayed there, and we talked. He pointed out how the evening wasn't a total disaster, reminding me my gown received many compliments and that I should consider the gown to be a beginning. 'It is your Picasso,' he told me."

"That must have been motivating. I love Picasso's art. Love his different styles."

"Are you an artist, Elena?"

"I've done some watercolors of Walter out in the snow."

"Will you show them to me sometime?"

"You really want to see them? They're rough."

"I thought that first gown I made was pretty rough, but people seemed to like it."

"You mean everyone except your date, right?"

"Yes. He never even noticed it."

"Such a loser."

"I sometimes wish I still had that gown."

"Where did it go?"

"I threw it in the trash."

"Why?"

"The gown reminded me of him."

"What a waste. It was your Picasso, Ivy."

"I thought so too. But he tarnished it. I now think my Picasso is the Winter Gown."

"The Winter Gown?"

"That's what I named the velvet gown that led to my being named Designer of the Year. It's not the title that matters to me. It's everything that gown represents."

"Like what?"

"Like your grandfather, his red cutter, playing checkers with him in the summertime, that house on the lane, my sister Izzie, Vivian and her shop, Murphy and his hot chocolate, my parents."

"Oh look," Elena whispered, as she aimed her phone toward a clump of trees. "There's the bunny that made all those tracks."

"You have good eyesight. I never would have seen that rabbit."

"She looked just like Pearl."

They kept going until the young photographer noticed deer tracks in the snow.

"I love Pearl and Walter. Especially when they are together. I think they make a lovely couple. That guy wasn't your type, Ivy. You didn't make a good couple. He was all about himself. I think the gown you threw away was your Picasso. It was the original. The first. That other gown was designed for a competition. The first one was designed by you with Vivian's guidance. It represented Gramps and his red cutter and the two of you playing checkers in the summertime and that house on the lane, your sister, Murphy and his hot chocolate, and your parents more so that the gown that earned you a title. Just my opinion."

Going around some brambles, Ivy thanked Elena for her input. "I appreciate your honesty, Elena. Your point is well taken. That first gown was the original despite its tragic demise."

"Think I could design dresses?"

"Whatever you create, you'll be creating Picassos in your own style."

"Really?"

"Yes, really. They might be watercolors or oils. Maybe they'll be books of poetry or songs played on a piano or sung by Bocelli or even breathtaking tapestries or unforgettable screenplays. Maybe, Elena, they will be a son, a daughter. There's so much we don't know."

A call for their attention vibrated through the forest. It was Doc. The tree had been found.

"We better hurry."

"Thanks, Ivy."

"For what, Elena?"

"For showing me the woods are so much more than just trees. They are a work of art."

Chapter Twelve

"There you two are!"

"We've had so much fun looking for a tree, Gramps."

"I'm glad to hear that, but the search is over, Elena. We are about to cut down this magnificent balsam fir."

"It's a beautiful tree, Doc, fitting for the last tree in your home."

"Thank you, Ivy. I agree."

Because Doc refused to use a chainsaw out in the woods, saying he didn't want to disturb the animals any more than they already were, it took a while for a handsaw to bring the tree down. He and Andy kept taking turns. But once it fell, out came the hot chocolate. When everyone had a cupful in hand, they raised them in salute to a most perfect Christmas tree.

"You're all invited to my home this Saturday afternoon for a tree decorating party and pizza starting around four. Now let's secure this beauty on the sled and head back. From those aromas, I could tell a wonderful meal awaits us."

Once the tree was in place, Andy asked Doc if he could drive the sleigh back to Ivy's.

"Take us in, Andy. The reindeer know you well."

As Andy was climbing into his seat, he glanced back at Ivy. From her smile, he knew she understood they were heading to the barn.

With a trace of snow still falling, the sleigh being pulled by the reindeer looked like a Christmas card, especially with the balsam fir following behind.

Approaching the farmhouse, Andy headed toward the barn. Doc reacted.

"Wrong direction. Turn them the other way."

Andy kept going.

"Slow them down. Turn them around."

With the barn feet away, Ivy leaned forward.

"Doc, we want to show you something."

As Andy pulled on the reins, Ivy jumped off the sleigh. Opening the barn door, she invited everyone inside.

"What a massive space, Ivy. From the outside, it looks smaller."

"I've been told that before, Doc. When I bought this place, I had dreams of raising sheep or chickens. I even wanted some horses at one point. But if any of that happens, it won't be for years. So, Doc, I would like to offer you this barn for your reindeer. They can occupy this space for as long as needed. Move them in anytime. This barn is yours in thanks for all those games of checkers and words of wisdom."

The wind whistled through the open door as Doc gathered his thoughts. It took him a minute. Santa is the one who is supposed to be bringing surprises, not receiving them. Holding Vivian's hand, Doc replied.

"'Thank you' sounds trite. There are no words to describe the relief I feel with your generous offer, Ivy. If at some point you change your mind, please tell me. I will understand. Having a herd of reindeer over-take your barn is no small undertaking."

"You don't need to do a thing, Doc. Water is hooked up. Heat is available. Bring in whatever else you use to care for them."

"Tell me what you need, Ivy, for a rental price, and I will write you a check."

"Keep your check, Doc. Merry Christmas."

The inviting aromas coming from the kitchen of the farmhouse welcomed everyone back from the woods. It didn't take them long to gather for another mug full of apple cider punch. Then Ivy took the pasta dish out of the oven and set it on a decorative ceramic tile in the middle of the dining room table decked out in a fine cranberry-colored linen tablecloth.

"Need some help, Ivy?"

"Yes, Elena. Could you please bring in the rolls sitting on the counter? They're in a wicker basket. Then the steamed vegetables sitting next to them?"

After Ivy placed the rice pudding on the table along with the rolls, warm banana bread, and steamed vegetables, then lit the candles about the room, she invited her guests to sit down. It was snowing again. Christmas was in the air.

"I know you say you never cook, Ivy, but everything is so delicious," remarked Vivian.

Everyone agreed.

"I appreciate your kind remarks, but Lawrence guided me along the way. That is, except for the rice pudding and banana bread. Those are the two recipes I know by heart. Both were my grandmother's recipes."

"I haven't had rice pudding in years, Ivy. It brings back so many memories," said Doc, taking another spoonful.

"I love that you've served the pudding in a Jewel bowl. I have a few that were in my family."

"This particular bowl was my grandmother's. I thought it fitting to serve her rice pudding in her bowl. I only remember a few family traditions. Bringing out this bowl over the holidays was one of them."

Conversation was lively. Quite festive. After the table was cleared and Ivy served the tiramisu with coffee, everyone rejoiced. They stayed, sitting and talking even after they'd finished their dessert. While enjoying their second cup, Andy's phone rang.

"Someone must be sick," said the veterinarian.

But that wasn't the case. It was his neighbor calling. There'd been an accident.

"I heard a truck go barreling down the lane," Tom explained. "A few minutes later, there was a commotion by your barn. All I could see was Walter. He was in the lane, Andy. The police are here."

"We'll be right there, Tom."

From the look on Andy's face, everyone could tell something bad had happened.

"It's Walter."

That's all Andy needed to say. Everyone was on their feet. Ivy got them organized.

"Leave the sleigh where it is. Put the reindeer in the barn. There's some hay in there and water. I'll drive my truck. There's room for six people. Put the tree in the back end, and let's go."

"We can't leave the kitchen like it is," said Vivian.

"Oh, we certainly can," replied Ivy, grabbing her coat and keys. "Let's get moving."

They flew back to town. No one said a word as Ivy turned onto the lane and parked the truck. They could see the crowd gathered and police lights whirling. Except for Vivian, they all went running down the lane. Tom saw them coming.

"From what I can gather, two trucks went barreling past the barn just as your rabbit was crossing to the other side."

Elena took off.

"Pearl! Pearl! Are you okay, Pearl?"

A police officer stopped her.

"It's my rabbit. Pearl is my rabbit."

By then, Doc was by her side. Together they pushed through the crowd. What they saw broke their hearts.

"Gramps. Look at Walter!" Elena sobbed.

They all had tears in their eyes as they looked at Walter in the middle of the lane, lying near Pearl, protecting her. If someone came near Pearl, Walter would let out a moaning sound even Doc had never heard.

"I know, Walter," said Doc, kneeling down beside the mighty reindeer, petting him, telling him how much he was loved while gently checking Pearl.

Doc kept talking to Walter.

"You were a good friend, Walter, a kind and loving friend. We will all miss our sweet Pearl. She was the plumpest, whitest, softest bunny I've ever known."

"Walter wasn't struck," Doc explained a few minutes later, to those gathered around him. "He's lying there to protect his friend from strangers. He knows Pearl was hit. He knows he has lost her. I'm sure Pearl passed instantly. There's not a bruise on her. She looks as if she is sound asleep."

"Oh, Gramps," sighed Elena, crying, as Doc took her in his arms. "I feel so sad. So sad for Pearl. So sad for Walter. Maybe if I'd stayed here, Pearl would have been with me instead of out here on the lane."

"Life is full of maybes, my Elena. The truth is, life just happens, and sadly what happens is sometimes tragic. Pearl always knew how much you loved her."

Wiping the tears from her eyes with her coat sleeve, Elena whispered, "I'll talk to Walter, Gramps."

Walking slowly toward the reindeer, she spoke in a soothing voice about his friend Pearl.

"You were lucky, Walter, to have had such a beautiful friend. I loved Pearl too. She was so soft and cuddly, and when I told her all my secret stuff, she'd wiggle her nose to let me know she understood. I think you probably do the same thing with me in your own way. I feel so sad for Pearl and for you. But listen to me, Walter. Pearl won't be far away. She'll always be in your heart. Now you must get up and get back into the barn. It's late. Gramps will take care of Pearl. Come on, Walter. Give Pearl a kiss good night. I'll wait here for you."

Walter stayed still.

"Pearl wouldn't want you to be out here in the lane all night long. It's too dangerous. Too many jerks don't watch where they are going. Soon you won't have to worry about that but right now, you do. So come with me. It's bedtime."

Walter didn't budge. Elena sat down next to him.

"I'll stay out here all night if I must. I can't lose both you and Pearl. So come with me into the barn and I will get you some sugar. Every little kid knows reindeer love sugar. So, let's go, Walter."

That got him moving. Gently nudging Pearl with his nose, Walter got back up and went into the barn. Elena was right by his side.

Doc turned to a police officer.

"When is something going to be done about this lane? It has become a speedway. Next time it might be a child that's killed. I know it won't be any of my reindeer. I am moving them out of here as soon as possible."

The officer wrote down everything that was said. Then he went to remove Pearl from the lane.

Doc spoke up. "I will take care of her."

Once the last police car drove away, Doc and Andy decided to put Pearl to rest out at Ivy's place. It was Ivy's suggestion.

"I'll be at home tomorrow until I come to help decorate your tree. You are welcome anytime. I am so very sorry for your loss."

"I think I'll go with you right now, Ivy. I'd feel better bringing the sleigh and reindeer back tonight."

"Whatever you think is best, Doc. We'll take Vivian home first."

"Elena and I will stay here until you get back, Grampa."

Giving Andy and Doc a hug, Ivy went inside the barn. Elena was brushing Walter, talking to him softly as he enjoyed some sugar.

"The hurt you feel when losing an animal you love is agonizing, Elena. The only kitten I ever had was hit by a car when we lived next door to Doc. He saw it happen. Picked her up and carried her down to this very barn. By the time he got inside, my kitten had died. I cried so hard I couldn't breathe. Doc put his arm around me, and we went back outside for some fresh air. He told me, 'You gave your kitten love, Ivy. That's the greatest gift you can give. Your pain will turn into beautiful memories. Just wait and see.'

"Doc was right. Now when I think of my kitten, I smile. I know she loved me. Pearl was blessed by your love, Elena. The happy memories you have will never go away. Doc's coming with me to bring the sleigh and the reindeer back here tonight. Your dad said the two of you will stay until Doc gets back."

"I'm not going to school tomorrow. I'll stay at Dad's tonight."

Ivy didn't feel it was her place to open that can of worms. Giving

66

Elena a long hug, Ivy walked up the lane to her truck. Sitting side by side, Doc and Vivian were talking.

"How's Elena?"

"She's mothering Walter between her tears, Vivian."

"That Walter has comforted so many over the years," said Doc. "While he's big and boisterous, he's really just a kid at heart."

"He takes after you."

"Well, you should know, Vivi."

Turning to Ivy, Doc added, "Change of plans. No need to take Vivian home. She's coming with me to your place, and then I'll take her home in the sleigh."

Vivian gave Ivy a wink.

"Sounds good to me, Doc. Don't you two get lost," said Ivy with a smile.

Driving up the lane to the front porch, Ivy stopped the truck long enough to help Doc get the tree from the back end onto the porch.

"I'll get that tree up first thing in the morning."

"Would you like me to come and help you? It's quite a big tree."

"I've put many a big tree up in that bay window, Ivy. It's only fitting I put the last one up."

So much happened in just a few hours. After Doc had the reindeer hitched up to the sleigh, he made sure Vivian was covered in blankets.

"Move a little closer, Vivi. We'll keep each other warm."

Laughter filled the December evening out in the countryside with woods full of Christmas trees, some decked in pinecones as the two lovers were on their way.

"See you tomorrow, Ivy," hollered Vivian.

"Have fun!"

"Ho, ho, ho. Merry Christmas, Ivy!" Doc bellowed as they headed across the field.

Waving goodbye until they disappeared under the moon, Ivy stood still for a few minutes, thinking how much those two traveling in a sleigh through the snow meant to her.

I've been so blessed to have you both in my life. Stay safe out there. You belong together.

Ivy kept thinking about Doc and Vivian as she cleaned up the kitchen.

I'm so happy to be home.

After wiping down the table, Ivy put the Jewel bowl back on the shelf. Then she went upstairs for the night.

A snow globe sitting on a small table next to Ivy's bed seemed to be glistening under the moonlight coming through a nearby window. It caught Ivy's attention.

When moving Ivy and Izzie out of the house on the lane, their mother had grabbed some stuff and thrown it into bags. While getting settled in the apartment, she tossed the bags into a closet and forgot about them. Years later, Ivy found the bags when looking for old family photos. Instead, she found the snow globe. It was hers in the first place. Doc had it all wrapped up for Ivy on one of their last Christmas Eves together in his barn. He surprised her with the snow globe after she'd helped him care for some little kittens found abandoned in a parking lot.

Getting into bed, Ivy took hold of the snow globe and shook it back and forth. As thoughts of a sleigh pulled by reindeer played with her heart, Ivy went to put the snow globe, with its tiny snowflakes swirling, back on the table. That's when she took a closer look inside the globe.

Ivy couldn't stop the tears.

She'd looked inside the globe many times when growing up. But this was the first time she noticed the little white rabbit standing between a reindeer and a decorated tree. This was the first time she noticed little pinecones painted on the branches.

Of course this is the time for me to notice the little white rabbit and the pinecones on the branches. I know that's you at work, sweet Pearl. Sweet, sweet Pearl.

Pulling blankets up around her, Ivy listened to wind chimes singing outside, eventually lulling her to sleep.

Chapter Thirteen

Up early, Ivy was online looking for a recipe with a mug of coffee sitting next to her. Problem was, she didn't know what kind of recipe.

Noticing an image of an old-fashioned woodstove on a website had Ivy thinking about her grandmother again. She'd heard stories of how the woman cooked using her woodstove. Everything she cooked was simple and delicious. Ivy felt like cooking something simple and delicious and consoling to offer those who would be coming with Pearl. Soups caught her eye. Minutes later, she had her recipe—a chicken soup. Checking the cupboards and refrigerator, all ingredients were in the house. Remembering what Lawrence said about breads and salads, Ivy found a boxed version of cranberry bread and a simple recipe for macaroni and cheese. She went to work in her kitchen.

A few hours later, the farmhouse was again filled with delicious aromas. Ivy decided she liked the feelings such aromas inspired. While placing soup bowls on the dining room table, Ivy noticed something on the floor. It was a pinecone. Thoughts of Elena and her dad came to mind as she hurried upstairs to get ready for the day.

Around nine thirty, as Ivy sat in her studio overlooking the back fields, contemplating designs for a new line, her attention was drawn to the swaying of pine branches out in the wind and snow. All sorts of branches seemed to be dancing about on such a splendid winter day.

Hemlocks swayed with spruce and evergreens as Fraser firs moved to the rhythm beside scotch pines and cedars. She'd been feeling the urge to take a bold step away from the usual wedding gown themes of lace and sequins but didn't know what that should be. Ivy started sketching. The more she sketched, the more the images took shape. She called Lawrence to discuss her ideas.

"Are you telling me you want a line of wedding gowns with tree branches embroidered on them?"

"I'm not sure what I'm after, but I feel something is there, right outside my window. I sat watching the branches move in the wind. Maybe that means using more chiffon or maybe layers of chiffon or maybe some organza, although I doubt it. That stuff is too stiff. Layers of chiffon would get that feeling of tree branches dancing in the wind."

"Layers of chiffon might be all you need, Ivy. Maybe the trick would be in the branding. Name one design something like the 'Evergreen.' Another, the 'Hemlock,' and so on. The difference could be where those layers are on the dress. Maybe embroider a hint of a specific branch somewhere on the dress or even on the veil. But I think just by using those labels, your customers would get the feel of branches flowing in the wind. Maybe on the label itself, include an artist sketch of the tree branch and a bit of copy about the tree. I feel the timing is perfect. The environment is becoming more and more front and center, which is a good thing."

"Maybe we could hook up with an environmental group protecting the trees."

Thinking about what she'd suggested, she changed her mind. "No, forget that. I don't want any connections with any groups. It can get too political."

"Smart. So, you could have various tree branch designs. Each would indicate the name of a tree. Good so far. What about an overall name for the collection?"

"I'm thinking of calling it the 'Elena Collection.' I was in the woods with Doc's great-granddaughter searching for his Christmas tree. Her name is Elena. I don't think she'd ever been in the woods for any amount of time. At first, she told me all the woods had to offer were trees. By the time we left, she told me the woods are a work of art. It was the way she said it, Lawrence, with such wonder in her eyes. It got me thinking. And when I looked up the meaning of the name Elena, I learned it means 'a bright, shining light,' and it all came together. That describes her perfectly. She could be represented as the sun on the labels."

"Once we get a marketing program behind the Elena Collection, those dresses will fly off the racks."

"I'd like to include Elena in all promotions if we move ahead with this. It's always smart to include a story about the beginning of something. That creates a connection between the brand and the public. That will be up to her. Of course, we'll give her a percentage of the sales."

"You nailed it again, Ivy. I love how all you need is a spark of an idea and the rest comes flowing out of you."

"I couldn't do any of it without you."

"By the way, sales for the Winter Gown are soaring. Some places run out of dresses minutes after putting them on the racks."

"That's tremendous news, Lawrence. We'll celebrate when I get back."

"Have you decided when that will be?"

"I'd planned on leaving Monday, but I'll have to wait and see. Things keep happening. Get this: I'm even cooking on my own. I got up early this morning and made soup and bread, from a box, and macaroni and cheese from scratch. In a strange way, I feel like I've found a family. It's an odd mismatch of characters, but what family isn't a bit odd?"

"I can hear the changes in your voice, Ivy. Did you enjoy going to the woods for a Christmas tree instead of asking me to search that huge closet for the box holding the parts to our tree?"

"I did enjoy being in the woods. It brought back so many memories. Some of them were sad but having Elena with me turned out to be a big help. That said, I did miss seeing you getting lost in the closet looking for the tree. I can't wait to catch up."

"Same restaurant? Same table in the corner?"

"Of course, Lawrence. I'll be in touch."

It wasn't even a half hour later when her guests arrived. Throwing on her coat and hat and pulling up her boots, Ivy flew out the back door, zipping her coat on the way.

"Good morning. How is Walter today?"

"Acting strange, Ivy," Elena remarked.

"I'm certain Walter's erratic behavior is due to losing his friend Pearl. Some animals sense loss," Doc explained. "They are aware something has changed, but they don't know how to react. Walter knows what happened. He was there. Now he no longer has Pearl to chase after or care for or go on walks with down the lane. We must be patient with him. Walter will adjust, just like we humans do when we lose someone we love."

"His reactions do sound almost human."

"Animals mimic us in many ways, Ivy," replied Doc.

"Pearl was very smart, just like Walter," said Elena. "She stayed clear of dogs and ran away from kids who only wanted to catch her. I will miss her forever."

"Don't lose sight of the fact you were very kind to Pearl. You earned her love. Those who insist the reindeer must be removed from the lane are cruel. They do not have a heart. Now, let's get down to the reason we are here. It is for Pearl. We will find a peaceful place for her to rest."

"It has to be under some trees, Gramps. Pearl loved stretching out under the trees in the summertime."

Going out to the truck, Doc took hold of a wooden box. Then everyone followed him down to a cluster of pine trees. No one said a word while Andy took a shovel and prepared a place for Pearl. Before putting her to rest, everyone took a turn saying goodbye. Elena was the last to speak.

"You and Walter will forever be my best friends. I could tell you anything and you understood. I love you, Pearl. I will come back, and we can talk some more."

After they said some prayers and shed more tears, Ivy invited everyone inside for a light lunch.

"I have a pot of homemade soup simmering on the stove as well as a loaf of cranberry bread and macaroni and cheese, if anyone is hungry."

That's all it took.

While walking to the farmhouse, Ivy told them to feel free to visit Pearl whenever they felt like it.

"I don't have to be here for you to visit. In the spring, you can plant some flowers. Maybe a tree? Maybe both? Whatever you feel like doing for Pearl, go ahead and do it."

Soon they were gathered around the dining room table once again.

"We didn't expect you to cook for us today, Ivy."

"I'm starting to like cooking, Doc. Today I was cooking in celebration of Pearl and the joy she bought to the three of you."

"Did your friend Lawrence help you this time?" Andy asked.

"No. I went it alone," laughed Ivy.

"What do you eat in New York since you don't cook?"

"Well, Elena, we order take-out or go to a restaurant around the corner from my studio. I can't remember when I cooked anything besides toast. But that might be changing."

"Change is inevitable. Soon we'll move the reindeer out of what has been their barn for years," said Andy. "It will seem strange to drive down the lane with all of them behind us in a hauler."

Doc changed the subject. "I'm thinking I'll go through the cubbyholes tomorrow if you still feel like helping me, Ivy. I have no clue what we will find. I've been chucking stuff in those cubbyholes for years."

"Anytime will work for me, Doc. What can I bring to your tree decorating later this afternoon? Take advantage of my newfound fascination with the kitchen."

"Vivian is bringing a tossed salad. I'm getting the pizza."

"I'll check with Vivian, Doc."

"When are you going back to New York?" Andy asked.

"Probably Monday or Tuesday. I'm creating a new line, and that citywide charity event is in early January, so I need to get back."

"What do you have to do for that event?" Elena asked.

"It's up to each individual business. This year we're hosting an open house at my showroom. Lawrence is making all the arrangements. We'll offer special pricing on some gowns. I still need to figure out what to auction off."

"Why not one of your wedding gowns?"

"I've done that for the last few years, and it remains an option for this year unless I can figure out something unique. I must tell you, Elena, you were the inspiration for the new line of wedding gowns I will be designing."

Ivy went on to explain. "I was sitting in my studio earlier this morning watching the wind blow the snow around tree branches. To me it looked as if they were dancing. Then I thought about our time in the woods together and your enthusiasm. I knew something was brewing, so I called Lawrence. We went back and forth, and from that came the beginning of a new line. It will be known as the Elena Collection. Individual dresses will be named after a certain tree, like the Hemlock, the Evergreen, and so on. Chiffon will be used to create the feeling of branches dancing in the wind. Graphics on the tags will play on the tree reference. The presence of the sun on the tag will represent you, as your name means bright, shining light. This is all in the preliminary stages."

"Wow! This is so exciting, Ivy!"

"Wait! There's more. With your permission and your parents', I'd like to include a little background on you in the marketing information that will be released before the line is unveiled. I can send you what that will be. You can delete whatever you chose or make suggestions of what to add. And of course, you will receive a percentage of the sales. This will all be conducted professionally through my lawyers. If you decide you do not want to be involved, I will understand."

"What a wonderful opportunity, Elena."

"I think so, too, Dad. Thanks, Ivy! Now I have to get my act together."

"And what may I ask does that mean?"

"I think I have to get serious about school, Gramps."

"You mean attend your classes?"

"Yes, Dad, and more."

"What do you mean by more?"

"I'm not sure yet."

"I heard you down in the kitchen late last night."

"I needed a soda. I couldn't sleep after losing Pearl."

"A soda?"

"Yes. I wanted some sugar. When I went back upstairs, I sat looking out the window just like you did earlier, Ivy. The stars were sparkling. That made me think of our talk about being a Picasso. I'll keep on doing my watercolors because I love doing it and the more I do, I hope to get better at it. I have a lot I want to do. I just have to figure it all out. But having a wedding gown line named after me, designed by a world-famous designer, is a pretty good start. And to think, it all started with a walk in the woods."

"I told you the woods are more than just trees. They are a wonderful place for inspiration."

"Remember, Ivy, woods are a work of art."

"I will never forget that Elena."

After enjoying what was left of the tiramisu with coffee, Doc made note of the time.

"I could sit here all day, but we have a tree to decorate and pizza to pick up."

"Another busy day, Doc."

"That it is, Ivy. And I'm so happy you are a part of it."

Elena went rushing out the door.

"Where are you going, young lady? We are heading back home."

"I'll be right there, Gramps. I have to say goodbye to Pearl."

Chapter Fourteen

After freshening up, Ivy called Vivian.

"So, tell me about your ride home in the sleigh."

"Before I go on and on about that, Ivy, I must ask about Pearl's burial. Was Elena okay?"

"Yes. Of course, she was sad. But she was quite happy where Doc decided to put her to rest."

"I always say the hardest part of having a pet is losing a pet."

"I agree. I told Elena about my kitten getting hit by a car, and as I did, I felt the tears coming back. You never forget. Now, tell me about your ride home with Doc in his sleigh."

"I felt like a teenager, Ivy. Doc is still such a romantic."

"Details, please. He seemed quite happy when I saw him earlier."

"I've been so careful to hold back my feelings over the years. I settled for a friendly relationship, thinking Sunday spaghetti dinners were all I needed. Thinking I could settle for being good friends. I'd tell myself I was too old. Or I was that other woman who never got her man. Despite the way he looked at me, he never offered a hint as to how he felt about me or about us. But last night, being in that sleigh, going through the snow bundled up in blankets under the moon, we let our guard down and finally—finally—we admitted our love for each other.

I felt alive, Ivy. Carefree. I forgot about being run over. All I wanted was him."

"What did he say?"

"We were getting close to the village when he slowed the reindeer down and told me we needed to talk. I thought it was about Elena or Andy because he talks about them all the time. But instead, it was about us."

"I bet you heart was on overdrive."

"It was, and even though we were sitting outside in the freezing cold, I was having hot flashes—and Ivy, I'm way past menopause. With his arm around me, Doc said that the thought of moving from that house has freed him of any guilt he may have had concerning our writing letters while he was married to another. He compared moving to turning a page in his life. He said he'd done the proper thing by staying married despite his wife kicking him out of their bedroom and never sleeping with him again after finding my letters yet refusing to let him go. When their son was killed, his wife told him that was God's way of punishing him for all his scandalous behavior."

"How did he go from one day to the next?"

"Having Andy saved him, as did his barn full of animals and eventually his beloved reindeer. He mentioned you as well, Ivy. When the two of you would play checkers, he told me it made him feel needed. When you moved away, he cried for a few days. Then he put the game away and never played checkers again."

"I had no idea his life was so miserable, and I lived right next door. He always seemed so happy."

"We all know people like that, Ivy. On the outside they're all smiles while inside, they're in anguish. Heck, that describes me for so many years."

"So why, after his wife died, why didn't he open up to you then?"

"Doc felt he needed to be there for Andy one hundred percent, especially since Andy had lost his father. But, Ivy, Doc told me it's now our time. Moving out of that house has given him permission to start over, to love and be loved."

"I am so happy for you, Vivian. Your love story is an inspiration."

"Thank you, Ivy. Before last night I'd talked myself into settling with the way it was instead of being the bold and brash version of me. Looking back, that's the way it played out. Looking forward, I feel like a schoolgirl in love with the hottest guy in the class."

"That is a wonderful feeling. I can't wait to see you later today."

After discussing what Ivy could bring to Doc's, they said goodbye.

Instead of going back to the kitchen to create something wonderful to eat, Ivy went to her studio and worked on sketches for the Elena Collection. Sitting down with sharpened pencils, pen and ink, and a sketch pad, Ivy connected with that creative thing inside her. Time flew. When she came up for air, Ivy jumped off her stool and grabbed her phone. She told Vivian she'd order a vegetable platter at the supermarket. Besides the platter, Ivy added an assortment of holiday cookies to her order. She never ate cookies during the year, but there was something about decorated sugar cookies in various Christmas shapes. She asked for extra reindeer. Just before hanging up, Ivy ordered more sugar cookies and had them shipped to Lawrence. His sweet tooth would be happy.

A little after four, Ivy pulled up in front of the yellow house on the lane. Looking through the sheer living room curtains, Ivy could see the Christmas tree standing in the corner. The lights were on. Sitting there for a minute, she thought about the Christmas she came running down the front stairs and found the desk her grandfather made her sitting under the tree. In the single drawer, she found that pad of paper and some sharpened pencils. It was one of those moments you never forget.

A knock on her window pushed that memory back in time. Looking up, there stood Andy, holding on to boxes of pizza.

"Hope you're hungry, Ivy. Grampa ordered every combination of pizza available."

"I'm starving. I hope you like Christmas sugar cookies."

"My favorites."

"How is Doc doing? It must be emotional for him, decorating the last Christmas tree in this home."

"He's fine. In fact, he seems jubilant. He just went to get Vivian."

Ivy wasn't surprised. *If he could, he'd probably be doing cartwheels.*

"I've been thinking. Would you like to go for a drink later? You'll be leaving us very soon."

"I'd love to go for a drink, Andy."

"Wonderful! That is wonderful!"

Walking up front steps she'd run up so many times excited to see Doc Armstrong, hoping he'd be able to play checkers with her, Ivy held the door so Andy could maneuver inside.

"The tree is huge, Andy."

"The bigger, the better as far as Grampa is concerned. I was here earlier to help him secure it. What a job that turned out to be. He's particular when it comes to his Christmas tree."

Putting boxes down on the kitchen counter, Andy took Ivy's coat as Elena ran through the back door.

"Hi, Elena. How is Walter doing?"

"He still seems so sad, Ivy. I feel the same way. Poor little Pearl. She was just crossing the lane. She did that all the time."

"It's a good thing Doc is taking the reindeer out to the country."

"I can't wait. Did you bring these cookies, Ivy?"

"Yes. Help yourself."

Grabbing a few, Elena thanked Ivy again for naming her proposed new line the Elena Collection.

"I did a few sketches before I came. Once I get with Lawrence, things will take shape pretty fast. You'll have to come to the city for the unveiling."

"Me?"

"Of course. You have a stake in the line as well."

"In in a way, I'll be a businesswoman."

"Yes, in a way. There will be stories published about you and the wedding gown line you inspired."

The back door flew open.

"Watch out, girls. I'm holding on to this beautiful woman and she's holding on to a tossed salad."

"No problem, Grampa. I'll take that from you, Vivian."

"Thanks Andy."

Giving Vivian a hug, Ivy remarked how radiant she looked. "It must be the freshly fallen snow."

"Oh, it must be," chuckled Vivian.

The house was busy. Earlier that morning Doc brought boxes of decorations in from the barn, so everything was ready to go.

"The lights are already strung," he explained. "Now comes the fun part. Small decorations go on the top. The larger ones go on the bottom. Ruth used to sit some of the bigger ones, like this stuffed bear, back in on a branch. She liked it when lights would shine on them."

"Grandmother was meticulous when hanging ornaments," remarked Andy.

"I see your name scribbled on the backs of many of these ornaments, Andy. Were they school projects?" Ivy asked.

"Most of them. Because I spent so much time here, my mother would tell me to hang them on Grampa's tree, so I did, every year. By the way, Mom says hello, Grampa. She'll be in town toward the end of January."

"Be sure to tell her we'll have our traditional dinner on whatever date works best for her. It will be the last time for another tradition in this house."

Moving closer to Vivian, Doc continued. "Next year, I will be in my new home, and I hope," Doc paused, "Vivian will be by my side as Mrs. Doc Armstrong."

Everyone stopped what they were doing. Most everyone was surprised when Doc knelt in front of Vivian and spoke from his heart.

"I don't have an expensive diamond to slip on your finger. I don't have youth to sweep you off your feet or tickets to take you away on a romantic honeymoon. What I do have to give is my love forever. I want to wake up beside you with the sunrise and go to sleep beside you in the sunset. I will respect you. I will cherish you."

Looking into Vivian's eyes—eyes that told their story from the moment they met at a soda fountain in the springtime of their lives to the winter now surrounding them—Doc spoke four beautiful words to the love of his life: "Will you marry me?"

There was no hesitation.

"I will marry you, my dearest."

Tears and congratulations flowed through that old house. Christmas came early. Ivy congratulated the happy couple, as did Andy and Elena.

"You both mean so much to me, Vivian. Choose any dress from my line, and I will have it ready, even if the wedding is next week."

"You don't have to do that, Ivy. Who knows? Maybe we'll elope. We've never talked marriage."

"Did I hear my bride mention eloping?"

"You did, my love. Ivy has been kind enough to gift me any dress of my choosing. I told her we've never discussed marriage, so even eloping is a possibility."

"Whatever we do, it will be perfect."

"I think we need to wait until you've moved out of here. Then we can start our life in our own place and make our own memories instead of being surrounded by others."

"See, Ivy, why I'm marrying this woman? We will get settled and then we will concentrate on our wedding."

Andy and Elena joined the conversation.

"Welcome to our family, Vivian. I am so happy for you and Grampa."

"Thank you, Andy," Vivian replied as Doc shook his hand.

"I'd like you to be my best man, Andy. Why should anything change? You've always been my best man."

"I love you, Grampa. Of course I'll be your best man."

Turning to Elena, Vivian asked her to be the maid of honor. "I realize we are just getting to know each other, Elena, but with your father as the best man, I think having you as my maid of honor will make the perfect beginning for all of us."

"I'd love to be your maid of honor! Thanks for asking me, Vivian."

Ivy made the same offer to Elena as she did to Vivian.

"Any dress, Ivy?"

"Any dress. It's up to you and the bride."

With the thought of a wedding swirling about, it took Doc a few minutes to turn everyone's attention back to the tree.

"Let's get busy, everyone. I know the thought of seeing me all decked out is exciting, but first things first. We have a tree to finish decorating and then some great food to enjoy."

Just as Andy was climbing up the ladder to put the angel in its place, there was a knock at the door.

"Ivy," Doc called from the kitchen, "could you get that?"

"Sure, Doc."

The porch light was on. When Ivy opened the door, a man was standing there, smiling. Ivy was sure he had the wrong address or a sick pet in need of Andy's attention.

"May I help you? This is Doc Armstrong's residence."

Before the man could reply, Vivian and Doc were on either side of her. That's when the man spoke.

"I stopped by, Ivy, to see if you'd like to have another cup of hot chocolate with me."

That's all the tall, well-dressed man with a warm smile and an Italian woolen scarf around his neck and hair a bit gray needed to mention. Ivy stepped onto the porch and embraced him.

"Murphy! What a surprise. How did you know I was here? Oh, I am so happy to see you again!"

"Let's go inside," Doc suggested. "I don't think we have any hot chocolate, but I can offer you a glass of wine or a cup of coffee. It's wonderful you could make it, Murphy."

Everyone gathered around the dining room table, with the tree in view.

"I think I timed my visit just right, what with all the pizza and Christmas cookies sitting on the table."

"You always were the planner, Murphy. Any meeting I ever attended with you involved went smoothly."

"We had some rambunctious meetings, didn't we, Doc? I miss this place."

"This place misses you. No one since has run that hotel like you did. Things keep going downhill."

"When I get back to Chicago, I'll give you a call, Vivian, and we can talk in detail."

"I would appreciate that. Thanks, Murphy."

"Last time we spoke, you told me you'd be coming for Christmas and staying with your brother."

"When we spoke, those were the plans, Ivy, but plans changed after Doc called to tell me you were here. He wasn't sure for how long, so I caught a flight and here I am. I also have some business to do downstate, so it all worked out."

"It's so sweet of both of you to make this happen. It's wonderful you keep in touch."

"Now we'll put you on our contact list, Ivy. We have lots of fun with it."

"I'm sure you do, Doc."

"Well, Murphy, I must let you in on something that happened earlier. Get ready for this! I proposed to Vivian. And, she said yes!"

"Congratulations! That is wonderful news! I'm not surprised. I've always thought you two belong together. This is the best news I've heard since my daughter told me she was getting married."

"Well, congratulations to the father of the bride!"

"Thanks, Vivian. To take this full circle, my wife and daughter went wedding dress shopping and came back with an Ivy Nolan Original Wedding Gown. Now her maid of honor and attendants are shopping for their Ivy Originals. It's a small, wonderful world!"

"Murphy, I am delighted to have such support. Please, tell the bride and her wedding party the gowns and any accessories are on me, with my sincerest congratulations."

"Ivy, your generosity overwhelms me, but I can't let you do this."

"It's done. I just texted Lawrence, and he'll take care of everything."

Elena spoke up as Andy brought more pizza to the table. "Ivy is designing a new line of wedding gowns. I gave her the idea, so she's naming it after me."

Ivy explained in detail.

"What a great story. I love stories of beginnings. You have come a long way since we first met, Ivy. I'm so glad I came. You all mean so much to me."

Murphy stayed for a good two hours.

Before leaving, he repeated more than once he'd be back for Doc and Vivian's wedding.

"Whatever the date or time, I will be sure to attend. You are proof that love is ageless."

Things slowed down close to ten o'clock. After dropping Elena off at her mother's, Andy and Ivy went for a drink.

"I think this will be the quietest place for a Friday night. They have a band. A good band and it's not a party crowd," Andy explained as they sat down at a table overlooking the river.

As they were ordering their drinks, a few of the band members stopped by to say hello to Andy, who introduced them to Ivy.

"I've been told you guys are pretty good," said Ivy. "I can't wait to hear you play."

"Maybe you can talk Andy into playing along for a few. He's still the best guitar player around."

Once the band was back on stage, Ivy asked Andy about his guitar playing.

"I had no clue you were so talented. When did you play guitar?"

"I played with a few of those guys in a different band, but I haven't played in years. I started in a band when I was a freshman in high school, but eventually I felt I should follow in my grandfather's footsteps. He'd been so good to me. My father was gone. There was no one else left."

Taking a sip of her drink, Ivy asked Andy if he missed playing.

"At times I do. Most people might think playing guitar in a band is stressful. I found it just the opposite.

"That's probably because you loved it, Andy. Most people think I'm nuts devoting so many hours into, what some say, is drawing a dress. I've stopped trying to explain it. If you're not wired that way, then you'll never understand." Pausing, Ivy asked, "Did your wife understand?"

Taking a good, long drink of his beer, Andy replied, "She couldn't understand why I quit the band. She supported my guitar playing more than my being a veterinarian."

"Really? Was that before Elena was born?"

"Before and after. She comes from a musical family. They all play an instrument. Susan, my ex-wife, plays piano."

"Did you ever play together?"

"Yes. One year for Christmas, we made a recording for family members."

"So, if you love to play and your wife plays the piano and supported you, why did you quit playing?"

"My grandfather had a bout with cancer at the same time my grandmother was in the hospital with pneumonia. She eventually passed away. I felt I owed it to my grandfather to devote whatever time I had to my career. I gave up the band and the guitar and I lost my wife and daughter."

"Has the thought crossed your mind that with the upcoming move it might be a good time to make some other changes? Your grandfather is retired. Maybe get a partner. Hire another veterinarian. Restructure so your hours are more flexible, giving you weekends off to play in a band. There is always a way."

"I've mentioned some ideas to my grandfather, but he goes on about losing my father and how hard that was for him and how much it means to him that I followed in his footsteps. So, I'm stuck."

"I don't believe we are ever stuck, Andy. Sometimes between praying and getting creative, things work out. Do you think Susan would come back if you started playing in a band again? Seems like that's what brought you together in the first place. I don't know Susan, but could she have felt you chose your grandfather over her?"

"I've wondered that myself."

"Did you go to counseling together?"

"She quit going after a few sessions."

"What was her reason?"

"She said she was tired of talking about it. Elena told me she has a boyfriend."

"Did you ask her?"

"No. We're divorced. She has every right to date. Even to get married."

"Or maybe you still love her and you didn't want to hear the answer."

Asking the waitress for another beer, Andy listened to the band, moving his fingers as if playing the guitar. And as he played, Andy replied, "Susan loved it when I played this song."

"It's a good one."

With the song over, Andy looked at Ivy, then he whispered, "I miss playing, Ivy. I loved everything about it."

"Then do something about it, Andy. This is your life. Not your grandfather's. And if you think about it, all he ever wanted was for you to be happy. He most likely has no clue how much playing guitar means to you."

"I never talked to him about the guitar."

"He is not a mind reader. He's a grandfather who also stepped into the role of father the best he could. All you have to do is open up to him. You'll find he understands."

With music playing in the background and a few people sitting at the bar and couples dancing, Andy changed the subject.

"Thanks for listening to me, Ivy. You've helped me put things into perspective. I will make some changes and talk with Grampa. But enough of me. I want to thank you for the attention you've given Elena."

"You are welcome, Andy. I've enjoyed our time together. She reminds me of myself. Off doing her thing with the animals. Teaching herself how to watercolor. Telling me the woods are a work of art. Your daughter is full of the wonder of the world around her. Don't feel guilty about your problems with Susan. Feel excited as to what lies ahead for Elena and for you."

"Having you name your new line after Elena was quite inspiring to her and to her mother and me. It has emboldened her to look beyond the boundaries of her hometown and see the world full of possibilities."

"Everyone needs reassurance. For me, it was Doc, Vivian, and Murphy. That's why it was important to me to give back. I've invited Elena to New York when the Elena Collection is introduced. Of course, you and her mother, as well as Doc and Vivian, are invited."

"Thank you again, Ivy. I'm not sure if you knew, but Doc told Elena and me that he was going to ask Vivian to marry him before he proposed to her. He didn't want his announcement to take us by surprise. To be honest, Ivy, it was obvious to me even at a young age that my grandparents were unhappy with each other. They led separate lives. Slept in separate rooms. I am so happy Grampa has found the love of his life."

"I am happy as well. They make a wonderful couple."

The dance floor was crowded when a fast tune was played.

"Watching everyone dance reminds me of my only trip to New York. I went with some guys I'd met in vet school. They were from New York. Took me all over the place. We ended up in some oldies bar. They only played fast songs, and many of the couples hardly ever sat down."

"I've never heard of such a place, but it doesn't surprise me. After all, it is New York."

"Tell me about the city. Do you find it easy to live there?"

"I do now. At first, I was overwhelmed. But once I got my bearings, I was fine. But it will never be home."

"Could you ever move back here?"

"Probably not in the near future. It's important I stay visible in the city. Competition is fierce. But I'm not that far away. We'll see. The train makes it easy, and I have Lawrence to cover for me."

"That man sounds indispensable."

"None of us are indispensable, but he plays a significant role in the business. I value his opinion. I trust him."

"Do you love him?"

Taking a sip of her drink, she simply asked, "Why does that matter?"

"I apologize, Ivy. It is none of my business."

"I try not to go there. What I do know is, I'd be lost without him."

"I get it. Elena told me the other day she'd never fall in love after watching her mother and I struggle and then battle with each other in the divorce. I tried explaining to her that when you get married, you never think it will end in divorce."

"What did she say?"

"She told me she'd rather take care of the animals. Their love is for keeps."

"Sounds to me there might be another veterinarian in the family, Andy."

"We'll see. Elena has many interests and many talents. I will encourage her to explore them."

"Although I've never married, I would agree with you that most people don't go into a marriage thinking it could end in divorce."

"That takes me back to Grampa. While my father's death devastated him, I've always thought if his marriage had been a healthy one, losing their only child would have brought my grandparents even closer. I don't mean to dwell on my grandfather, but my gut tells me he has been in love with Vivian for a very long time. I get a sense there's some history to that relationship. It didn't start with their Sunday night spaghetti dinners. That's just my observation, Ivy. And really, it is none of my business. Grampa deserves to be happy."

Ivy offered no information. She kept the reason Andy's grandmother kicked Doc out of their bedroom to herself. It was not her place to tell him anything.

"Doc has earned the happiness he has found with Vivian."

"Speaking of being happy, Elena told me this morning she wants to get another rabbit once her grandfather moves off the lane. She thinks that will make Walter happy."

"Your daughter is what my mother used to call her supervisor at the hospital—one heck of a spitfire." Ivy laughed at herself, adding, "I don't know where that came from."

"Maybe something triggered your memory since we've been talking about stuff in the past. Let's get back to the present. Would you like to dance, Ivy?

"I'd love to, Andy."

Not many were dancing to the slow tune.

"They left the floor to us, Ivy."

"That's a good thing. I can be clumsy."

"I'll hold onto you. I won't let you go."

Just as Andy was about to take Ivy's hand, the music stopped. The drummer took over, getting everyone's attention. Then the lead singer spoke.

"Folks! I have a surprise for you. With us tonight is about the most talented guitarist around. If we give him a hand of applause, maybe he'll pluck a few strings for us. What do you say, Andy Armstrong?"

The lights were dimmed even more as a spotlight was put on Andy. People started clapping and whistling and calling out his name. At first Andy refused the invitation. Then Ivy encouraged him.

"Go for it, Andy. This is what you're all about."

Giving Ivy a hug, Andy joined the band. He looked like a natural standing up there, treating the acoustic guitar snug in his arms with respect. After some going back and forth with the band, Andy stepped up to the microphone as the lead singer made an announcement.

"Okay, folks! You're in for a treat. Here's Andy Armstrong playing a favorite of yours and mine, 'Horse with No Name.'"

From the minute Andy played the first chord, the audience was on their feet as the lead singer sang those familiar words. At one point, Andy took that song off on his own, injecting his own version with his own take on the chords and the feel of the song, interpreting it to the point that people wanted more from this guitarist. Andy did not disappoint. It was obvious he was in love with the moment, the guitar, the people, and the feel of the strings against his fingers and the guitar in his hands. He ended the moment with a crushing version of bits and pieces of songs most everyone knew by heart.

That pub by the river was rocking.

Andy was in demand. But he ended it, thanking everyone, as well as the band. Then he stepped down off the stage. It took a few minutes for the place to quiet down. Some came over to shake his hand. Some asked for his autograph. One particular woman recognized Ivy. She made sure everyone heard her.

"It can't be! I read online that you were from here, but I never expected to run into you. Listen up, everyone. Standing next to Andy

Armstrong is the New York City wedding gown designer Ivy Nolan. She's from here. Used to live in the yellow house by the lane not far from downtown. What an amazing couple!"

More people came buzzing around them. They both signed autographs and heard stories about favorite wedding gowns and favorite songs and favorite designers and guitarists. The lead singer eventually broke it up.

"Okay, folks. One last round of applause for Andy Armstrong and his friend, designer Ivy Nolan."

The reaction was deafening. Once the band began playing a slow song, the crowd quieted down. As Andy led Ivy to the dance floor, a woman stopped him.

"Andy! I loved hearing you play."

"Susan! So glad you caught the song."

Then Andy introduced Ivy to his ex-wife.

"I'm happy to meet you, Ivy. Elena goes on and on about you. She's so excited with your invitation to the city. You have been such a role model for her, especially after naming your upcoming line of wedding gowns after her."

"I'm pleased to meet you, Susan. I've enjoyed spending time with Elena. Her creativeness and love of nature and animals inspired me just when I needed some inspiration. Did Elena tell you I plan to invite you and a guest as well as Andy and a guest and a few others to New York in January? I'll be sending Elena the details."

"Thank you for including me, Ivy."

"Of course, I would include you, Susan. You are Elena's mother."

The two hugged.

"Phil and I were just leaving. He's that tall guy paying the bill. I had to tell you, Andy, how good it was seeing you and hearing you play the guitar. It has been too long."

"Andy told me you are a gifted pianist. That's wonderful that you recorded songs for your family. Maybe when I get back here, I can listen to it."

"That would be fun, Ivy. I'm so surprised Andy told you about our CD."

"From what he said, Susan, I could tell it meant a lot to him."

They said goodbye.

Taking Ivy's hand, Andy led her around the dance floor.

"I hope you didn't find that awkward, Ivy."

"Not at all. She's a lovely woman."

Andy kept dancing. "Did you see that Phil guy she was with? He has slick black hair. That's not Susan's type. Not at all."

"I wouldn't have a clue, but I do think you are a very good dancer."

"My grandmother insisted I take lessons. She'd say girls don't like boys who can't dance."

"So, you must jitterbug too."

"I do them all, Ivy. But dancing with a beautiful woman like you is my favorite dance."

Pulling her closer, Andy moved about like Fred Astaire. Ivy relaxed. She couldn't remember the last time she'd been held by a man on a dance floor. It felt wonderful. Like melting in the heat on a hot summer day. She'd been so absorbed with wedding gowns that she hadn't come up for air in ages. Now, dancing about a pub sitting alongside a river in the wintertime with snow falling, Ivy closed her eyes and let her guard down, and when she did, her thoughts were no longer focused on lace or satin, not even on designs or awards. Her thoughts were all about Lawrence. Those guardrails were destroyed, and there was Lawrence, front and center. As Andy swirled them and led them around and around, Ivy admitted to herself she was attracted to Lawrence—sweet, kind, handsome, funny, determined Lawrence with a keen eye for business, a creativeness for design, and an affection for fabric and netting as well as a skill for cooking and a shyness she realized she adored, along with his unruly chocolate-brown hair and ever-present smile.

With the lights dimming, Andy slowed the pace down. It was the last dance of the night. Gently, slowly, Andy kissed Ivy on the cheek, and then moved his lips to hers as the moon spread over the snow-covered landscape. Lost in the moment, Ivy responded until the lights came on and the song was over. Still, they lingered, caught up in emotions that took them by surprise.

"I didn't mean for that to happen, Ivy."

"I didn't either, Andy, but I'm glad it did."

They kept lingering, holding hands on the dance floor as tables were being cleared.

"What do we do now?"

Ivy paused before answering. "I think it is best if you take me to Doc's so I can get my truck. It's late. Tomorrow is the day I go through those cubbyholes with your grandfather."

It wasn't long before Ivy was back at the farmhouse. She was tempted to call Lawrence but decided what she had to say merited a dinner for two at their favorite restaurant. In bed, with blankets snug, Ivy thought about the evening, the very slow dance, and her Fred Astaire partner.

She would forever treasure his leading her about the dance floor and that kiss—a kiss she would never forget.

Chapter Fifteen

Ivy was up early the next morning working on sketches for the Elena Collection. To get in the mood of swaying chiffon, Ivy considered walking out to the woods to hear the wind move through the branches but time was limited. Doc told her if she was at his place by eleven, they'd be able to go through all the cubbyholes and decide what to do with whatever they found. Knowing how difficult it was for Doc to let go of stuff, Ivy doubted they'd get through all the cubbyholes, especially if they were interrupted. She was certain they would be.

As Ivy was getting out of the shower a little before eight, her cell phone rang. She knew who it was.

"Good morning, Lawrence."

"Morning, Ivy. How'd your evening go?"

Where should she begin? Making a quick decision to skip over the dancing part, she talked about Murphy showing up.

"What a great surprise, Ivy."

"There will be more surprises today when Doc goes through those cubbyholes. I plan on making a list of the stuff he'll be keeping. That way when he moves, he'll be able to keep it all organized."

Lawrence had another call. "Do you know when you'll be getting back home so I can reserve our table?"

"I'll be getting in Tuesday around four."

"See you then, Ivy."

Realizing there'd be heat in Doc's barn, Ivy slipped on a pair of jeans and a comfortable sweater. She'd bring along a scarf, some mittens, and a pair of boots and wear a down-filled jacket she'd found on sale at Macy's. Ivy thought about the times when the heat went out in the yellow house and her father would swear all the way down to the basement to see what was going on. She and Izzie would stay in their beds covered in blankets.

Putting her hair back in a ponytail, Ivy pulled her toque down over her ears and headed out the door. Cleaning snow off the truck and letting it run for a few minutes, Ivy looked beyond the fields to old barns weathering yet another winter.

It looks like a painting. Oh, the stories those old barns could tell.

After stopping at the grocery store for some snacks and waters, Ivy was on her way back to the lane. Her first stop was Doc's house. Going around to the back door, Ivy was about to knock when Andy pulled up.

"There's my dancing partner," he smiled, getting out of his SUV.

"I enjoyed our evening together, Andy. I can't tell you the last time I went out for a drink."

"It might be hard for you to believe, Ivy, but I can't remember the last time I went out for a drink. By the time I finish for the day, the thought of going back out is a bit too much."

Noticing Doc's footprints leading to the barn, Andy added, "It looks like he's already out there. I'll be around later to rescue you with some coffee. Elena will be here at some point. She had something going on."

"Take your time. I know Doc will be telling his stories."

"I'm sure he will."

"I am the lucky one, Andy. See you later."

"Ivy?"

"Yes?"

"Thanks for listening to me last night. I hope I didn't sound like a crybaby."

"Not at all, Andy. You have a lot going on."

Leaving her truck parked in the street, Ivy walked down the lane as thoughts of taking Izzie for walks before suppertime came to mind They weren't allowed to go beyond Doc's barn.

It turned out to be a brilliant Saturday. Snow squalls moved further down the river. When Ivy opened the barn door and walked in, Doc was sitting nearby with a pile of stuff in front of him on the floor.

"Good day, Ivy."

"Good day to you, Doc. Starting without me?"

"No. All of this belonged to Pearl. I want to gather it together so nothing gets lost in the move. I've never known a rabbit to have toys, but thanks to Elena, Pearl had many."

"Andy told me Elena wants to get a rabbit once you move to the country."

"Oh, that girl! I'm not surprised. I'm sure she'll add a puppy and kitten to the list as well. Not complaining. She has a heart of gold, just like you, Ivy. I talked to Andy earlier. He said you two had a wonderful time last night."

"We did. Your grandson is quite the dancer."

"His grandmother insisted."

"Are you a dancer?"

"No. No, I am not a dancer, and that never went over very well with Ruth. But nothing ever did."

"Just think, Doc. You're about to embark on a new chapter in your life with Vivian."

"You don't think I'm an old fool, do you?"

"I think you are a lucky man. Vivian is quite the catch."

"I was out getting the paper earlier and ran into my card-playing friend, Nate. I told him I was getting married. Told him who the lucky lady is, and that Nate had the nerve to tell me he had his eye on Vivian. Said he'd asked her out a few times, but she always turned him down."

"From what I know about both you and Vivian, I think you're the perfect match."

With all of Pearl's belongings packed into a box, Doc led Ivy to the wall of cubbyholes.

"Funny to think remnants of a life are stuffed into cubbyholes, but here we are. It started when I'd be busy. I'd tell myself I'll just put it here for now, whatever it happened to be. This will be interesting to see what I considered in too good a shape to throw away."

"Maybe you'll look at some of it and wonder why you kept it in the first place."

"That's what I'm hoping, Ivy, especially since I'm moving to a new place with my lovely bride. Let's get started."

"My thought is, we organize the stuff you decide to keep. I brought a pen and pad of paper to write it all down. The rest you can put in one area for the trashman."

Doc was anxious to get started.

"Be careful on that ladder, Doc."

"Under control, Ivy."

But the process became a challenge. Doc found it hard to let go.

"While I'm thankful I've sold the property, there are just so many memories here. I guess I'm a sentimental old fool. I've lived a long life and most of it in this barn, loving every moment and remembering every animal that came through the door. You see those notches in that old board? Every notch indicates another birthday for my son, my only child, Eddie, when he was growing up."

"Doc, can I ask you something personal?"

"You are like a daughter to me, Ivy. You can ask me anything."

"When your son was killed, how did you carry on?"

"I felt responsible for helping take care of Andy. I knew Eddie would have wanted me to do that, so I did. Ironically, Andy was Eddie's only child. I was protective of him. I still am."

"You are a strong yet gentle man, Doc."

"Funny thing about losing a child, Ivy. While obvious milestones like Christmas and birthdays are crushing, so is having no reason for first days of school or filling Easter baskets or going to a parade on the Fourth of July. But even harder, Ivy, even harder are the littlest things. The smallest things. The everyday things. For me, it was the smell of bread toasting in the toaster. Seeing that jar full of stones collected on walks down the lane sitting on a shelf or a little cup put away for good or finding a book that I read every night before bed, usually more than once, and when he was sick, I'd read it until he fell asleep. And when he fell asleep, I'd still worry. I'd always worry. Was I a good father? It can eat you up if you let it. My boy was an adult when I lost him, but he was still my boy."

"How did you work through all that pain, Doc?"

"I know Vivian told you about our writing love letters. At some point after losing Eddie, I began reading those letters, over and over sometimes."

"From what Vivian told me, I thought your wife kept those letters."

"She did, but Ruth drank most every night after we lost Eddie, and one night she told me where she kept them. She told me I'd never have them. When she fell asleep, I went in her room and took my letters back. The next morning, I told her I had them. Told her they were my property and if she had a problem, she should call her lawyer."

"Did she?"

"No. She had no fight left in her."

Doc took a minute before continuing.

"So, it might sound odd, but when I read the letters, I felt at peace. I felt hopeful. If two people, meaning Vivian and myself, were physically so far apart yet so very much in love, I realized I could still love my boy like I always did, as if he was near, sitting on my lap or skating on the ice rink we made behind the barn. Loving Vivian brought me back to living. Loving her took away the bitterness."

Looking out a window, Ivy noticed it snowing. Not hard. Quite gently for the conversation going on.

"Let's take our time with the cubbyholes, Doc. We have all afternoon."

In the process of taking their time, they found lots of interesting stuff. Some stuff, Doc forgot he had packed away.

"Well, look at this. I thought Ruth threw it out and here it is, right where I put it."

"I repeat, be careful on that ladder."

"I'm coming down, holding on to history."

With the box opened, Doc explained. "These newspapers and magazines published over the years represent times in our history we should never forget—everything from Kennedy's assassination to the fall of the Berlin Wall to Nixon, The Beatles, and so much more. History is an ongoing story. That's what I used to tell Andy and his father. I'll put the box in the back room. Before I move, I'll donate it to the library."

"Nowadays, you could sell them on the internet and make some good money, Doc."

"I'd rather make all of it available to the general public."

They kept on going. A box way back in a cubbyhole brought Doc to tears. "Eddie's hockey skates he wore over the years. Oh, those early mornings, cleaning snow off the car so I could get inside and warm it up before Eddie and I hit the road for a practice or a game. He loved hockey. He was a smart player. I'll give the box to Andy. Let him decide what he'd like to do with all of it."

"Did Andy play hockey?"

"He did for a while, but he didn't like it. Didn't like getting up early like his father did. Didn't like the cold. Didn't like all the practices, whereas Eddie never missed a one. He'd rush out the door as if every practice was his first practice. Eddie was a people person. Anyone who knew him loved him. He played for Boston College, studied to be a lawyer, graduated with honors, and was hired by a prestigious Boston law firm but never had the time to build a career. He and his wife, Karen, moved here just before Andy turned three. They thought it'd be easier to raise him in a small town. Eddie was excited to come back home. He figured he'd open an office downtown. He did everything right, Ivy. He was a good son, good husband, and father."

"Were you surprised he chose law over becoming a veterinarian?"

"When it was time for Eddie to select a school and a career, I told him I'd support whatever path he chose. His then to-be wife was accepted at an Ivy League school in the Boston area, so I figured that was the reason he went there. He was head over heels in love with her, Ivy. Between you and me, I think he chose a career that would guarantee him good money so he could afford her taste. She comes from one of those New England families. You know. They have a bloodline full of accomplished men and women dating back centuries. I'm sure he felt he had to prove he was worthy not only of her but her family as well. And my son did just that. I was so proud of him."

"I'm sure you were very proud of him, Doc. Does Andy remind you of him?"

"I can't say I've thought much about that. Maybe in the eyes he does. The way he smiles. It's a crooked smile. Always makes me laugh. Oh, they both had freckles. Eddie was the funniest kid. He'd try to wash his freckles away. Now that I think about it, Andy always seemed a bit needy. I don't mean that in a bad way. He just needed more of my attention. I felt as if I had to lead him along a little more. Eddie was more independent."

Taking a breath or two, Doc went back to the ladder.

"That's enough of my rambling on. We'll be here for weeks if I keep it up."

The pace of going through cubbyholes increased. After taking out the bells worn by the little reindeer and the card Ivy left for Doc and putting them on his desk, they got down to work. Along the way Doc discovered old parts to sleighs and bikes and parts belonging to one red cutter. He found photos, so many photos, of Eddie as a baby, Eddie going to school, playing hockey, growing up. That cubbyhole took some time getting through. He discovered leashes and old 45 rpm records, even autographed photos of famous hockey players. He laughed when he discovered some fishing lures.

"I thought I'd enjoy fishing. So, one day I went out and bought myself a pole and these lures and went fishing in a boat with a buddy of mine. We used to play cards with a bunch of guys every other Thursday night in a small room at the diner. We'd take the room over and eat all the time we were there, so they made good money off us. Of course, some of the guys had too many beers. So, anyway, I went fishing with this card-playing buddy of mine, and the first cast he took got caught in the back of my head. I ended up in the ER, and these things ended up in a cubbyhole."

Not needing a ladder any longer, Doc grabbed a box from another cubbyhole just as Andy came through the door carrying coffees.

"You are a savior, Andy, with those coffees."

"Here you go, Grampa."

Handing Ivy hers, Andy asked how it was going.

"We're making progress," Ivy replied.

"Will you look at this? I have no clue where these came from."

Pulling some tissue paper out of a shoebox, Doc reached in and held up some folded pieces of paper and a diary.

Ivy jumped up and took a closer look.

"Those are mine, Doc. Those are mine!"

Ivy took hold of the folded papers and the diary. A bit in shock that they'd been found, she sat back down and talked about the items in her grip.

"Remember when you went with me on my tour of the yellow house, Andy? Remember before we went inside, I told you about the closet in my bedroom in that house and how I kept stuff hidden under a floorboard in the closet so Izzie wouldn't find any of it? I told you how our mother moved us out of that house when we were in school one day, so I never got to go back to my room. I never got to go into my closet again, so all the stuff I had in there, I considered to be lost."

Holding up what was obviously a diary, Ivy continued. "This is my very first diary. For some reason it was in a cubbyhole all that time and so were these. This is the strangest thing. How did my very first sketches end up in one of your cubbyholes, Doc?"

"Just as you were telling that story, Ivy, something clicked. When the people who bought the house from your mother were moving in, they found those things up in what was your bedroom. Having children themselves they realized someone might be looking for the stuff. I happened to be walking down the lane one afternoon when the man stopped me and told me what he'd found. I suggested he leave what he found with me. The next day he came with this stuff. I kept it out for a while in hopes you'd come around. Eventually I put it all in the cubbyhole thinking I'd take the time to try to find you when I had the time. I must have forgotten about it. I'm so sorry, Ivy."

Doc hurried out back to another room, a much smaller room full of more stuff.

"Ivy! Come out here."

Holding on to the diary and sketches, Ivy followed. So did Andy. They found Doc pulling an old tarp away from something underneath it. Ivy hurried to make sure what she was seeing was her old desk.

"It is! It really is my old desk. Oh, it is my desk! My grandfather made it for me one Christmas. He left me a pad of paper and sharpened pencils in this drawer. In this drawer right there. I kept the desk in my closet so I could sit and draw my designs with no one around to bother me, meaning Izzie. Did that same man bring my desk to you, Doc?"

"Yes, it was the same man. I can still see his little head with his big mustache. Yes, it was him. I remember the man telling me how the desk was so well made. After he left, I moved it in here, back in the corner out of the way, and covered it up. Again, I thought you might come around, and again, I forgot about it."

"What a great story. Makes me wonder what else you'll find."

"There aren't too many cubbyholes left to go through, Andy, and that's a good thing. It's getting to be dusk out there."

In walked Elena. She started right in.

"Mom told me you two met last night, Ivy."

"We did, Elena. We had a very nice conversation. I made sure to tell her she was invited to New York next month."

"Dad, Mom said you played the guitar, up on stage. I didn't know you were that good."

"Your father had the people on their feet and clapping."

"I wish I could hear you play."

"Maybe we can make that happen, Elena."

"Mom told me you used to play in a band."

"I did."

"That is cool. Why did you quit playing?"

"I never realized you quit the guitar. Why?" Doc asked.

"I didn't have time for it after a while. Now come on, you two. Keep working. It looks like only a few more cubbyholes to go."

Those few cubbyholes didn't take long to clean out. There was nothing too exciting to be found.

"Remember those tins you just pulled out, Grampa? Grandmother kept them on a shelf in the kitchen. I wondered where they went."

"I sure do remember them, Andy. I'm the one who put them in the cubbyhole. I always thought they were the ugliest tins I'd ever seen."

Everyone enjoyed a good laugh until Andy drew their attention to the very top row of cubbyholes.

"Look," he pointed. "There's one more to go."

Doc was about to head to the ladder when Andy told him to stay put.

"You've done enough climbing. I'll get it."

Andy was up the ladder in seconds.

"It's really lightweight," remarked Andy, holding on to the ladder with one hand while trying to get a good hold on the box with the other. But the tape was old and yellowed. The top flew open. Andy lost his grip and the box went flying, crashing on top of an enamel cabinet and then rolling off onto the floor. It landed upside down with sheets of old tissue paper strewn about the area.

"Did anyone get hit?" asked Andy, down off the ladder and more embarrassed than anything.

Everyone had survived the fly-away box. It ended up in front of Elena, who was standing next to Ivy. Elena reacted. Bending down to pick it up, Ivy stopped her.

"Wait, Elena," she whispered, as memories of that terrible night at the downtown Grand Hotel came rushing back..

So many hurtful memories, leading her to ripping off her gown and heaving it in the trash. Then, grabbing hold of her bag, she hurried out of that lonely room, leaving the door wide open, the key in the lock, running down the stairs and rushing out the front door into a snowstorm. A night she thought would be magical, turned out to be repulsive.

That was the last time she'd seen that original emerald-green velvet gown. She assumed it'd been destroyed until standing inside a barn going through cubbyholes filled with memories.

When that fly-away box landed, Ivy could see a bit of a sleeve of a green velvet gown. She knew it was that gown she'd adored. After all, she'd designed it. Fell in love with it and worn it with pride as she walked down the wide stairway of the Grand Hotel into a ballroom decorated for the holidays on the arm of a young man who turned out to be nothing but a liar.

Ivy couldn't hold back the tears as she pulled the gown out of the box, declaring to those gathered in the barn, "This is my gown! This is my original velvet gown."

Taking a closer look, Andy explained, "That's the gown I found in a wastebasket at the hotel downtown."

"This is the gown I told you about, Andy. Remember? I told you after that creep dumped me, I ran upstairs and threw myself on the bed and went to sleep. And when I woke up, I took the gown off, this gown right here, and threw it in the trash. What were you doing there, picking through the trash?"

"I was sixteen or seventeen. I'd played in the band that night so I was there when that idiot pulled his stunt on you. Now I remember seeing a young woman running up the stairs when we were playing the last song of the night."

"That was me! But why were you up in that room, going through the trash?"

"I played gigs there quite often. I got to know Murphy's assistant. Sometimes he needed help getting the rooms cleaned up for the next day. He paid me to go around and make sure the wastebaskets were emptied because the trashman came early in the morning. I'd go back around 5 a.m. and help him out. That room number was on the list I picked up at the front desk, so I was just doing my job."

"But why did you take the gown out of the trash can, Andy? And how in the world did it end up in one of Doc's cubbyholes?"

"I almost left the gown in the trash until I took a closer look. Something told me not to toss it out. Something told me there was a story in that gown, so I brought it here to Grampa's. He was right over there caring for a puppy. Instead of bothering him, I found a box, folded the gown, put it in the box, wrapped it up and secured it, climbed the ladder, put it in a cubbyhole, and forgot about it."

"Oh, thank you, Andy, for saving this gown. I can't tell you what it means to me," said Ivy, embracing him. "This was my first attempt at a design, and Vivian was the seamstress."

"Is this the original, Ivy?"

"Yes, Elena, this is the original Winter Gown."

After finding a hanger for the gown, Ivy hung it out of the way on a nail in a backroom. Then she and Elena stepped back and took a good long look at a miracle.

"Not one rip or blemish. The gown is in wonderful condition," Ivy remarked, giving Elena a hug.

"It's very pretty, Ivy. It even looks like an original."

Doc and Andy joined them.

"I must say," smiled Doc, "finding that gown is the fitting end to going through cubbyholes. Let's get to the house. Vivian's been cooking her delicious spaghetti and meatballs with all the trimmings. We can sit and talk more about our findings."

The others followed Doc as he continued talking.

"It's another busy day tomorrow. Moving reindeer from one barn that has been their home to a new barn will be interesting."

"What time do you want to move the reindeer tomorrow?"

"Let's get it done in the morning, Andy. You can help with the move. Then I'll stay and get them settled."

"Please remember to treat that barn like it's your own. If any problems come up, call me and I'll take care of them."

"You're an angel, Ivy."

"You are the angel, Doc. Can you all wait a second? I forgot my gown."

Chapter Sixteen

The only light in the small space was coming from the moon streaming through the window situated behind the gown, making the velvet glitter like the snowflakes gently falling. Standing there, thinking about the moment she designed the gown, something moved outside. As the stars seemed to be frolicking about the evening sky, Walter peeked in through the window. The image of that massive reindeer with the moon above him and the stars glistening around him and that green velvet gown back where it belonged stirred her imagination even more.

That was the moment Ivy answered the question bothering her since being named Wedding Gown Designer of the Year. That question was part of the reason why she'd come home in the first place. Something was missing, she'd told herself after receiving the award. Something was lacking. Something was left undone. What was it?

There, hanging in front of her in an old barn about to change hands, was the answer—a simple yet stunning velvet gown–the original Winter Gown.

Staying still, as the barn creaked and a little puppy bedding down for the night yawned, Ivy was filled with the realization that the gown was only part of the answer. There were other pieces to this story, and every one of those pieces was gathered together under the moonlight—her diary kept when just a young girl, hidden from her younger sister, her first pencil sketches of fancy gowns, designed on lined paper and a pine desk made by her grandfather, her most treasured of all Christmas gifts.

They were all loose ends. All missing pieces of her beginning, all back where they belonged. All proof that Ivy Nolan was quite deserving of the title bestowed on her. She'd been working on it since sitting at her desk in a closet sketching designs. She'd been working on it since opening a door and a little bell announced her arrival at a fabric shop for the very first time. Now she had those pieces. Now she felt deserving. She felt it in her heart.

Elena interrupted the moment.

"Are you okay, Ivy?"

"I'm overwhelmed to have this gown back in one piece. I thought it decayed somewhere in a trash pile."

Taking it off the nail, the two joined the others waiting by the door.

"I hope I haven't made you wait too long."

"Not at all, Ivy. We never mind waiting for a friend."

"Thanks, Andy. I think you should know I saw Walter wandering around out back."

"Walter loves to wander, Ivy. That keeps getting him into trouble."

No one said another word. Instead of heading toward the house, the three went the other way down the lane.

"Are we going for a walk?"

No one answered Ivy.

When they were beyond the barn, they stopped. Then they turned back facing the barn, and there was Walter, prancing under the moon.

"Walter would like you to follow him, Ivy. Reindeer are smart. I'm certain he senses you will be leaving us very soon."

Ivy didn't understand, but then she wasn't tuned in to reindeer like Doc, so she handed her gown to Elena and started to follow Walter, who was way ahead of her now.

Ivy hurried.

That's when she noticed something written on an old board with nail holes around the edges. It was secured to a post about buried in a snowdrift. Thanks to the light from the moon, Ivy was able to read what it said, and when she did, she took a deep breath.

Ivy was going down the Mitten Path.

With tears running down her cheeks and that brilliant, beautiful moon showing her the way, Ivy walked down the path with the snow crunching under foot, going by mittens, all sorts of mittens hanging from branches, strung along as if they were on a clothesline, mittens resting in snowbanks, tacked to fence posts. Some had become warm little beds for little birds. Some were attached to another by a string. Mittens were everywhere. All different colors. So many different designs. Bunnies passed her by, as did squirrels and chipmunks, sensing something special was about to happen.

And then, it did.

Coming down the Mitten Path was a little girl hopscotching along with her yellow braids zigzagging about under the stars. The precious little child was smiling and waving as she skipped alongside an old red cutter with a little one inside wrapped in blankets, being pushed by a young woman with hair the color of Ivy's and tears running down her cheeks. As the woman and the cutter and the little girl with yellow braids zigzagging about got closer, the woman stopped the cutter and whispered in the little girl's ear. Then the woman tucked blankets around the youngest, kissed her on the cheek, and stood for a second looking at Ivy. Wiping tears away, she began walking toward Ivy. Walking turned to running toward Ivy with her arms outstretched just like a little girl, just like she used to, going down the lane with her big sister as the moon kissed the night and the stars shimmered like diamonds.

"Ivy! Ivy! It's me, Izzie! Ivy, I've missed you so."

Walter stepped aside. Even Walter knew this was a moment to be remembered along the Mitten Path.

The sisters embraced. Then they sobbed, and then they started laughing, just like they used to do when playing on the sunporch in that yellow house.

"Izzie! Oh, Izzie, you are a beautiful young woman. I've missed you so!"

"You'll never know how much I've missed you, Ivy. I received your messages. I tried calling you back a few times, but I'd hang up right after dialing your number. Don't ask me why. I'm so sorry. It could have been the fact that so much time had gone by. Maybe I was afraid it might have been too much time. I know that makes no sense, but my stomach is full of butterflies right now."

Holding on to Ivy's hands, taking a deep breath, Izzie continued. "I have followed your career. I am so proud of you, Ivy. So is Mom. So is Dad. They send their love."

Ivy felt like a little kid begging for her parents' attention and when she gets it, she doesn't know what to do with it.

Pausing, thinking of the good times they'd shared, Ivy asked, "How are they, Izzie?"

"Pretty good, Ivy. Dad had some health issues that made him realize if he wanted to keep on living, the drinking and the cigarettes had to go. So far so good. Mom is retired. Oh, get this, Ivy. Our mother, the nurse, started baking, and it's kind of taken off. She has a website. Even a blog, and she loves it, Ivy. And people love her. She has lots of followers. Dad told her she has your creativeness. They are very proud of you, Ivy. We all are so proud of you. Being here with you, a sadness I've felt has gone away. Now I realize that sadness was my missing you."

Hugging her little sister, Ivy spoke softly as another little bird flew by.

"I wish I knew why we stopped communicating, Izzie. For me, it was easier to walk away than to deal with all of it. I wrapped myself up in my wedding gowns, ignoring something gnawing at me. Ironically, I figured out what that gnawing was about an hour ago. Then I walk outside and discover you, Izzie, coming down the Mitten Path. All the pieces fit. My absence never meant I didn't love you or Mom or Dad, because I do. I always will."

"I will always love you as well, Ivy. I've grown closer to Mom and Dad, but it hasn't always been easy. I didn't go to school after high school. Instead, I worked at the diner for a while. That's where I met a guy who introduced me to drugs. That was all I needed. I took off with him. No money. Nothing. Slept my way with anyone he wanted me to just to get high. That all came crashing down when I found myself pregnant and on the street at twenty-one. I went into labor at eighteen weeks and lost the baby."

Izzie took a breath before continuing. "I showed up one rainy night on Mom's doorstep. Lucky for me she set some rules before letting me back inside. One was to go to college. It took a few years, but I ended up in nursing school. Graduated as an RN in obstetrics. I owe so much to Mom. She kept me moving forward when I felt like quitting."

Noting tears in Izzie's eyes, Ivy took her little sister in her arms, telling Izzie about the time she had food poisoning and their mother traveled to New York and stayed with her until she was released.

"Mom and Dad did their best, Izzie. That's all any of us can do."

"That's why I work in obstetrics. Once I was straight and sober, it became clear to me that I wanted to save babies, not neglect them. I will never forget the baby I lost. I felt all along that baby was a girl. I named her Angel because that is what that precious baby will forever be in my heart."

The sisters hugged a little more until the littlest one bundled in blankets in the red cutter started crying.

"Are those two beautiful little girls your daughters?"

"Yes! When the oldest one learned that we were stopping to see you for a few minutes, she got so excited. I've shown her your website and some articles about you in magazines. Come with me, Ivy, and meet your nieces."

If ever there was an early Christmas gift, meeting precious little nieces on the Mitten Path was the best.

"This is Louise, Ivy," Izzie said, smiling, with the youngest in her arms.

"Named after Mom's grandmother?"

"Yes. I've always loved that name. And this is Hazel, named after my husband Teddy's grandmother."

"Your husband! When did that happen?"

"We met at the hospital. Teddy's an obstetrician. I worked with him for a few years before going out with him. We were married six months later."

Kneeling in front of Hazel, Ivy told the little girl with yellow braids how much she loved her pretty hair and her name and her pink snow-suit. That's all it took. They were friends for life.

"Watching you two has made me so happy," said Doc, coming down the Mitten Path.

"It's all because of you, Doc," said Izzie. "When I picked up the phone and heard your voice, I was right back here on the lane."

"Whatever you did, I am so thankful for this surprise, Doc," said Ivy, smiling and hugging them both.

Elena and Andy joined in. Izzie couldn't believe Andy was so tall. So grown up with a beautiful teenage daughter.

"We have so many stories to share," said Izzie. "But I'm afraid we can't get into them tonight. There was a death in Teddy's family, so we're on our way to his parents. Let's exchange emails and all the rest. I promise to keep in touch. We only live three hours away."

"I'll say goodbye to you here, Izzie, as I have to bed down some reindeer for the night," said Andy, giving her a hug. "It was such a nice surprise seeing you again. I'm sure Grampa knitted all those mittens just for tonight."

"You know better than that." Doc smiled. "But your daughter did do some of the knitting."

"Thank you, Elena. You helped to create a moment I will never forget."

"You are welcome, Izzie. It was fun. I love surprises."

Pushing the little red cutter with Louise bundled in blankets up the lane, with Doc and Elena surrounding her, along with Ivy holding Hazel's hand, Izzie looked over at the yellow house with tears in her eyes.

Ivy embraced her little sister. "I know. I feel the same way. Andy and I took a tour of the house a few days ago. That's another long story, Izzie."

"I loved that house. I still miss it."

"I miss it too, Izzie."

When they reached the SUV, still running, Izzie made the introductions. Teddy was holding a baby.

"Three children! What a beautiful family, Izzie."

"Thanks, Aunt Ivy! Meet your nephew. Willie is five months old."

The smell of Ivory soap and sugarplums melted Ivy's heart. "He is precious, curly red hair and all."

"He takes after Teddy's side of the family."

"You must be so busy."

"Teddy keeps me organized and on time."

"I'm so happy we've met, Teddy."

"The feeling is the same, Ivy."

"One last thing, because I know you have to get going. I'll get a hold of Santa Claus to see what I can buy Willie, Louise, and Hazel for Christmas. I'm sure they've been very good."

"I am always good, Aunt Ivy. I would like a doll with lots of hair and doll beds and doll blankets."

"Thank you, Hazel. I will see what I can find. Love you, Hazel, very much."

"I love you too, Aunt Ivy."

Ivy couldn't speak for a few minutes. So, Hazel did.

"Aunt Ivy, Louise tries to be good. She needs a doll with lots of blankets, too."

"Thanks, Hazel. What about Willie?"

"He cries all the time."

"Okay," Izzie laughed. "Time to go."

Goodbyes were said and promises made again. As they pulled away, Ivy asked why there has to be endings.

"Because," Doc explained, "if you didn't have endings, you'd never have beginnings. Let's go enjoy some spaghetti."

With her arm wrapped about Doc's, Ivy kept thanking him for bringing Izzie home to the Mitten Path. Elena followed, holding on to an original velvet gown.

"What a most magical surprise. How wonderful. How very wonderful is that!" Ivy exclaimed as they walked by the yellow house on the lane.

"I'm an aunt," Ivy told the universe, standing under the stars. "How sweet is that! How very sweet is that!"

Chapter Seventeen

VIVIAN HAD PLATES AND NAPKINS ON the table and the spaghetti and meatballs ready to be served when they walked through the back door. Once they were all around the table, the conversation began as Vivian's fine cooking was enjoyed.

"You're going to spoil me, Vivi."

"I hope so, my love."

"Just think, Grampa. This is Walter's last night in his barn."

"While Walter thinks it his barn, Walter shares it with others."

"True, Gramps, but he is the ringleader."

"Oh, Elena! That describes him perfectly," laughed Doc.

"How do you think the reindeer will adjust?" Ivy asked.

"Walter just lost Pearl and now he'll be losing his home that has meant so much to him. Walter is a homebody. He's the oldest one out there so time will tell. The others will be fine. Walter is again going to learn, like we have, that nothing is forever, except for my upcoming marriage."

"You are such a romantic, even when you're eating."

"You bring the best out of me, Vivi."

Conversation flowed until there was a knock at the back door.

Andy jumped up. "I'll get it."

Opening the door, he was surprised to find Susan, standing there.

"Mom! What are you doing here?" Elena asked

Doc stood and welcomed her. "Whatever brings you here, Susan, you are always welcome. You are family. Come in. There's plenty of spaghetti if you are hungry."

"Thanks, Doc, but I've eaten. I brought you a gift for your new home. I want you to know I enjoyed the times I spent here with all of you."

"Why don't you stay for a while, Susan? That is, if you don't have plans."

"No. I don't have plans, Andy. I'd love to stay if you don't feel I am interrupting."

"Listen, young lady. Anyone who is thoughtful enough to bring this old man a gift is more than welcome. Please, have a seat. Elena, get your mother a drink."

After introducing Vivian and telling Susan they were getting married, Doc kept on talking. "Funny you should stop by. I've been thinking about you and Andy, and I have a few questions. If it's none of my business, just tell me."

Ivy knew what Doc was up to. She sat back and watched him go to work.

"Now, I'm an old dog, and you know what they say about old dogs and new tricks. It takes me a while to catch on to something."

Doc turned his attention to Andy.

"You told me you quit playing the guitar because of lack of time. I understand you played the guitar last night and were well received. I never asked about your guitar playing, Andy. I always asked your father about his hockey playing. I never encouraged you in any way. In fact, I took your life over, and I'll tell you why. Not that the why made it the right thing to do. It was my reaction to losing my son, your father. When Eddie died, a part of me died with him. To survive, I grabbed hold of you like a leech. I smothered you. Used you to ease my pain. Instead of helping you, I hindered you. Without saying it, I expected you to become a veterinarian. I never expected that of Eddie."

Taking a drink, clearing his throat, Doc continued. "Andy, this is your moment to make any changes you feel like making. You call the shots, and whatever you decide, you have my love and support. What the heck. Go join a band. It's never too late, boy."

Turning to Susan, Doc added. "Don't blame Andy for decisions he made that may have caused a problem in your marriage. I was a bully, Susan. I was outraged I'd lost my only child. The pain was crippling, but that is no excuse for smothering Andy. Your marriage and your divorce are none of my business unless my business interfered with yours. One thing I can say with certainty, I know you both loved each other. There. I said all I have to say. After I take my lovely Vivian home, I will come back and go to bed. Moving reindeer is a daunting task."

Ivy headed home about an hour later with a green velvet dress draped over the passenger seat and a diary and sketches right next to it. After having a cup of tea and watching some useless TV to unwind, she went upstairs to bed, but she couldn't get to sleep. When the phone rang, she was certain it was Lawrence. But it was Elena. Ivy thought maybe she called about what Doc had said, but she never mentioned a word of it. Instead, she wanted to talk about something they'd discussed in the woods searching for a Christmas tree.

"After seeing that original velvet gown earlier, I came home and read more about Picasso. He led a tortured life, Ivy, and still he created masterpieces. His paintings weren't tainted by any of that. They were inspired. Your inspiration that created the first green velvet dress was not tainted by what happened at the hotel. If anything, it made the dress even more enduring. It's nice to have everything shiny and new and perfect like the velvet dress that earned you that award. But I've learned shiny, new, and perfect don't last. It's being tainted by life and how you rise to the moment that matters. That green velvet dress we found today packed inside a dirty old box has earned the right to be called a Picasso. That's all I have to say. Except I have to tell you, Mom and Dad are out having a drink—together."

Ivy had to gather her thoughts. The wisdom Elena projected was that of a scholar.

"When considering your reasoning to conclude what you have, I must say, I agree with you, Elena. You bothered to do the research to prove your point."

"I now have a Picasso hanging in my closet."

Ivy paused before asking Elena her thoughts about her parents going out for a drink together.

"When they first divorced, I was angry with both of them. But after listening to Gramps, I understand them a little more. I'm not blaming Gramps. He was very sad and hurt. I'm finally not blaming anyone. If what Gramps said tonight helps my parents, then I'm happy they are having a drink together. If anything comes of that, it would be wonderful. If Picasso could create masterpieces while being surrounded by a torturous life, anything can happen. But if it doesn't, that's between the two of them."

After saying good night to Elena, Ivy had no problem falling asleep.

Those busy bird feeders woke Ivy up early the next morning. She stayed in bed for a little while listening to the snow buntings and chickadees, thinking of everything that had happened in the past week that felt more like a year. Ivy was overjoyed by Izzie's visit, meeting her family and catching up. The Mitten Path was enchanting. Thanks to Doc and Elena, it was just as she imagined a mitten path to be. Finding the green velvet dress stored away in a cubbyhole in Doc's old barn was nothing short of a miracle.

Checking the time, Ivy pulled the blankets down and hurried to the shower. She had reindeer coming to stay for a while.

Ivy was dressed in an instant, with her hair brushed, makeup on, and hot coffee in her cup. Scrambling some eggs, Ivy decided she needed some avocado toast as well. Sitting at the dining room table where the view inside and out was spectacular, Ivy thought about Lawrence, and the more she did the more she realized she had no clue what their relationship was about. Yes, they both were creatively driven. Ivy a little more so. They talked design and fabric and ideas all the time, and Ivy enjoyed every minute of it. They worked together. Closely together. Lots of late hours. There had been some nights where exhaustion led to sleeping together, but come the next day, they were back at work. Nothing was said about feelings or commitments. It wasn't like a relationship. It was more like a routine. Work hard all day and part of the night. Get together. Release the stress. Say good night and go their separate ways. But now that they'd been apart for a little while, Ivy stepped back and took a look at what was going on. Oh, the sex was good, but she didn't miss him in that way. She never liked the way he rubbed her legs with his toes or how he licked her fingers thinking it would arouse her, but honestly, it annoyed her. And then there was his falling asleep as soon as they finished. He'd be snoring before she got down the stairs.

Ivy could never stand the shoes he wore. None of them. They were loud. Some were shiny, but they fit the atmosphere surrounding them. Many associates thought Ivy and Lawrence were an item. Not with those shoes, Ivy wanted to shout up and down Madison Avenue. But he kept her organized. Their talks about their designs were invaluable. Most important, Ivy trusted Lawrence.

The image of the velvet green dress hanging in the barn with Walter standing in the window behind it came to mind. The more she thought about that, the more she realized that over the years she'd liked their relationship just as it was with no strings attached. But now, thinking about it, Ivy confessed she didn't want to keep up whatever was going on. Her curiosity of him when slow dancing with Andy was just letting her mind wander. Finding that velvet dress changed her. Maybe it wasn't just the dress. Maybe it was a combination of Doc and Vivian declaring their love after years of keeping it locked away and Elena describing the woods as a work of art or her reason why that first velvet dress was the original or maybe it was finding her sweet, sweet Izzie on the Mitten Path where the word *aunt* became personal. Or, maybe, just maybe, it was being home again.

Whatever it was, Ivy now looked at finding the sort of love that sweeps you off your feet with just a look or a touch; the sort of love Vivian found that day in a soda fountain to be what Ivy wanted in her life. Commitment took on a whole new meaning to Ivy Nolan named Wedding Gown Designer of the Year at the Plaza in New York City.

Getting up from the table, Ivy called Lawrence. She kept it short. She had to get to the barn.

After the small talk, he asked what time she was getting in. "Perfect. I'll secure the reservation."

Ivy wasn't going to tell Lawrence about seeing Izzie until she was back in the city, but she couldn't keep it in.

"That's wonderful, Ivy. What a great surprise. And now you know you're an aunt. Such lucky kids."

"I think they're all coming to the big event in January."

"Speaking of January, we're getting great response to our lineup of events. I just need to come up with something for the citywide auction."

"I'll think about it on the train."

Ivy could tell someone was driving up her road.

"I think Santa is arriving, Lawrence. The barn will soon be full of reindeer. Imagine that!"

Ivy paused before telling Lawrence she missed him.

"Yup. Bye, Ivy."

That was all Ivy needed. There'd be no more wondering about Lawrence's feelings toward her. No more sleepovers. Strictly business from now on and, of course, brainstorming for the next great design or collection. Lawrence was at his best when brainstorming, and that was why Ivy loved him so.

Grabbing her gloves and jacket and a few boxes of donuts, Ivy walked out the door to greet her guests, even those soon to be living in her barn.

The weather forecast called for occasional snow flurries and wind. Ivy hoped it wouldn't spook the reindeer. The barn creaked every time the wind picked up. After putting the donuts in the barn, Ivy went back outside as Andy was parking the hauler as close to the barn as possible.

"Good morning, Ivy. It's a great day for traveling with reindeer down a highway."

"I can't imagine! They probably haven't budged far from that barn since they moved in."

Elena jumped out of her father's truck.

"Hi, Ivy!"

"Good morning, Elena. I'm so glad you came."

Doc pulled in behind Andy.

"Morning, Doc. Welcome!"

Ivy waited for him to get out of his truck. Then she gave him a warm embrace as she whispered, "You did a wonderful job last night talking to Andy and Susan."

"I have you to thank, Ivy. I hope what I had to say did some good."

"Between you and me, Elena told me they went for a drink last night. It's up to them now."

"We can only hope. So, how are you doing? Ready to go back?"

"It's bittersweet. I've had such an amazing time this past week. You topped it off with the Mitten Path and getting in touch with Izzie. I'll never be able to thank you enough."

"You thank me every day with all your accomplishments and now, offering us this barn. One more thing. Vivian told me again about that good talk you two shared. It helped her get some things straight. Whatever you said, it worked a miracle."

"No, Doc. You are the miracle. I hope you and Vivian can make New York in January. I'd love for you to meet Lawrence and see my studio."

"Lord willing, we'll be there. Now let's discuss my use of this barn. I can't let you pay all my expenses."

"If you can't do that, keep the reindeer in the hauler and take them back to the lane."

"You're as stubborn as Vivian."

"That is a compliment."

Ivy turned her attention back to Elena. "Did you have breakfast?"

"I had a slice of toast. Dad came early. He had to talk to Mom."

"If you're hungry, I put some boxes of donuts in the barn. Help yourself."

"I will. Thanks. Are you packed yet?"

"Not yet. Since I keep clothes here, I don't have much to pack. I'll be coming back more often now that I've made some very good friends."

"I hope so," said Elena as they walked into the barn.

"And what are you hoping?" asked Andy, on his way out the door.

"Ivy said she's coming back more often."

"Well then, I hope so too."

118

Calling Elena to the hauler Andy asked her to take Walter for a walk.

"He knows what's going on. I think he needs some air."

"No problem, Dad. Want to come, Ivy?"

"I'd love to."

Once Walter was ready to go, Elena suggested they take him to see Pearl.

"I think he senses Pearl is near," she added. "His head is down. He is sad."

Sure enough, as they approached where Pearl had been buried, Walter stopped. Then he bent his head down again as if praying. Ivy and Elena stood on either side of him as the morning sun wrapped them in early sunshine.

Elena went closer to Pearl. Then she knelt down. Lifting his head, Walter shut his eyes and took in the fresh air.

"He smells something."

"Pearl?"

"I can tell he already knows Pearl is here. It's something else."

They both looked around. It was Ivy who solved the mystery.

"I know what Walter smells. Over there. Those are witch hazel bushes. They blossom in the winter."

"Oh, Walter! I think Pearl would love to play under those lovely smelling bushes, and I bet you were thinking the same thing."

They took their time walking Walter around. When they returned to the barn, there was a surprise waiting for Ivy in the back of Andy's truck.

"We brought you an early Christmas present. We didn't have time to wrap it." With that, Doc pulled off a tarp covering the desk Ivy's grandfather had made.

Ivy was overjoyed to have that desk back in her possession.

"Thank you so much for bringing this desk home to me," said Ivy as she ran her hand along the pine boards.

"Moving the reindeer inside your barn wasn't as hard as I thought it would be. We're finished for now, Ivy. I'll drive the truck up to your house, and Grampa and I will get the desk inside just where you want it."

Getting the desk through the front door didn't take long. Ivy knew where she wanted it.

"Perfect," she smiled. "It fits right underneath those bookshelves."

After hugs and more hugs, the friends began saying their goodbyes until the conversation turned to Walter.

"Please remember, the barn is yours for as long as you need it. If there are any problems, get in touch with me."

"I can't foresee any problems, Ivy, other than Walter, and there's not much we can do but pamper him."

"Do you think he's sick, Doc?"

"He'd been acting tired for a while, but since losing Pearl, he seems to be in a slump. We'll keep track of how he handles the move. As I've said before, all the reindeer out there in the barn are up in age. Walter is the oldest. He's approaching twelve, which is old for a reindeer. A change like a new location could prove traumatic."

"What can be done to make him feel hopeful again?" Ivy asked.

"Keep him as comfortable as possible and make sure he's eating."

"What if that doesn't work, Doc?"

"We have a plan if we need one." Doc explained. "Walter comes from a place way up north. His mother was found far out in a wooded area, alone, severely injured, and pregnant with Walter. When the two men who found Walter's mother brought her to Noelene's reindeer clinic, Noelene told them she was doubtful the mother or the calf would make it. Miraculously, both survived. And both thrived under Noelene's care. Throughout the process, Walter was with his mother. It happened to be a downtime for reindeer emergencies, so Walter and his mother had that barn mostly to themselves. The love shown to him from his mother and from Noelene and her staff left a lasting impression on Walter. Just as the house on the lane will forever mean home to you, Ivy, that barn way up north will forever mean home to Walter. Home remains in one's heart forever."

"How did Walter end up in your barn, Gramps?"

"It's a long story, starting when a woman stopped me in the grocery one morning to ask if I made house calls, explaining her horse needed my services. I was at her place within the hour. She remains a good customer and even more important, a good friend. She asked me one day if I favored any particular animal. While I told her I loved all animals, I admitted my intrigue of reindeer. That's when she told me about Noelene. It turned out that woman and Noelene are cousins. One thing led to another, and I was talking on the phone with Noelene about Walter. She explained that once she feels a reindeer is strong enough, she makes a decision about what to do with the reindeer. She told me most are able to go back to the woods, but Walter had never been without his mother. Never been on his own out in the elements, so Noelene was looking for the right person to care for Walter in a place he'd feel safe. I eventually proved to her I was capable and willing to bring Walter into my life and care for him in the way she would take care of him. My being a veterinarian was a plus, as was her cousin vouching for me. After I earned Noelene's trust, I was on a train going north to pick Walter up. We bonded immediately."

"You went by train?"

"It's the only way to get in there."

It was quiet on the steps of that farmhouse. Elena wiped her tears away as her great-grandfather continued.

"Reindeer get old just like we do. They need certain comforts just like we do. Noelene offers that comfort to all the reindeer under her care. They are a family."

"But Walter has us. We are his family. We should be taking care of him. Walter would miss us."

"Oh, but Elena, a reindeer seeks to be with other reindeer if at all possible at the twilight of their life."

"But we have other reindeer, and all the reindeer are old just like Walter."

With his arm still around Elena, Doc explained. "But that barn way up north is home to Walter. It holds dear memories. By just the smells and the way the wind moves about it, that barn will offer Walter the quiet and the dignity he has earned. That is where I will take him when it is time. Walter and I have been together for over a decade. I want his final days to be peaceful. Life is a gift, and Walter has lived it and spread his wonder to so many."

"When is Walter leaving?"

"That is up to Walter. He'll let me know. One more thing. The last time I spoke with Noelene, she told me there are rabbits living nearby. They visit the reindeer. She feels rabbits offer the reindeer a particular solace that only a rabbit can. I told her about Pearl and Walter."

"I'm so happy Walter will be home and there will be rabbits there to comfort him," Elena said, with more tears in her eyes.

A little while later, Ivy stood on the front porch of her farmhouse, waving goodbye to some very special people.

Then she went inside to get ready for her return to New York City on Tuesday

Chapter Eighteen

As Ivy PREDICTED, THE TRAIN RIDE back to the city was just what she needed to get some ideas flowing. She didn't know why that almost always happened when traveling by rail. She was just thankful that it did.

As that renowned skyline slowly became visible, Ivy had a thought. What would she wear to dinner? They'd gone to that restaurant so many times, but tonight she felt like dressing up. The first thing she did back at her apartment was take a long bath. She made sure to add extra flower petals and rosemary. Her plan was to stop at the showroom first, then go to the restaurant. It was just around the corner.

With time ticking, Ivy chose a simple black sheath, high-heeled pumps, and a tight-fitting jacket. She prayed it wasn't snowing. It felt wonderful to be doing something with her hair and to take time with her makeup and wear her pearls. She loved her pearls. Finding her small dress purse, Ivy tucked the necessary items inside and turned out the lights.

Off she went to meet Lawrence.

Unlocking the door of her showroom, the familiar scents welcomed her back. But there was one that was new. Lawrence had added Christmas trees to the mix. They were real ones. Beautifully decorated.

After checking on some things, Ivy was back out the door in her high heels with snow falling, heading around the corner to table number eight in the back.

For a Tuesday, it was quite busy.

"Good evening, Ms. Nolan. Your table is ready for you."

"Thank you, William."

Once he'd seated Ivy, William asked, "The usual, Ms. Nolan?"

"Yes, please."

Looking about the room, Ivy shook the snow off her fancy heels. She saw many familiar faces. Some nodded and waved a little wave. Ivy did the same in return. A funny thing happened: Ivy realized she didn't know any of their names.

Watching a waiter serve bowls of soup made Ivy think of her farmhouse and cooking her chicken soup and the way the snow piled up on the windowsills. She wondered how Walter and friends were doing in the barn. She thought about how she'd lay in bed, listening to the trains pass by across the river and wake up to see the sun rise over the horizon.

"Ivy? Did you hear me?"

"I'm sorry, Lawrence. I was thinking about cooking in my farmhouse."

Ivy changed the subject.

"It's so nice to see you, Lawrence! I've missed you."

"Missed you too. It's been busy." Lawrence sat down.

"It's that time of the year when lots of people get engaged," Ivy explained.

After they ordered drinks, Ivy asked, "Anything new with you? How are your parents?"

"My parents are fine. I was home for dinner the other night. They send their best to you, Ivy."

"Tell them thank you. Did you have your usual dinner special?"

"Actually no, Midge wanted to order a pizza, so that's what we had, and then, of course, we enjoyed some tiramisu. I thought of you, Ivy. You look lovely in that black sheath, by the way."

"Thank you. I felt like dressing up. So, tell me, who's Midge? I've never heard you mention her before."

"I met her at the Institute. I don't think you know her. She worked in LA and just moved back to the city because of a promotion." Lawrence was playing with his fork.

"Midge and I used to go out," he explained. "We used to be pretty serious, but when she moved that was the end of it. At least that's what I thought."

"What do you mean?"

"I mean I thought it was over. We both moved on. End of story."

Ivy couldn't figure Lawrence out. She'd never heard about this Midge person. She decided to find out more. "Thanks for the real Christmas trees in the showroom. Your thoughtfulness means a lot to me, Lawrence."

"It was strange not having you around, Ivy. When Midge and I went looking for the trees, I realized I hadn't done that since I was a kid."

"Sounds like you and Midge had fun."

This time he was playing with his knife, too. "To be honest, Ivy, we fell in love all over again. You know when you feel something is missing in your life and you have no clue what that is until it's staring you in the face? I've been perfectly happy working with you. Happy with our arrangement, I'll call it. I will admit I was attracted to you, Ivy, but I realized you were deeply committed to building your brand and I was okay with that. I understood and respected you for going the distance. I decided I'd wait in the wings. That is, until I saw Midge walking through the door. I realized love doesn't wait. It knocks you off your feet. It makes your stomach ache and your tears fall. All that happened when we looked at each other once again. Midge was what was missing from my life. When I held her, I felt whole. Last night I asked her to marry me. I will forever love you, Ivy."

Lawrence wasn't playing with his fork or his knife anymore. He looked relieved. He looked very happy.

Holding his hands in hers, Ivy congratulated Lawrence.

"I am so happy for you and Midge. I can't wait to meet her. She must be very special to have won your heart. To be honest with you, Lawrence, I came back from spending time with people I love realizing what you and I shared wasn't the sort of love that you and Midge share. It was convenient. You know. We worked hard. Enjoyed each other for a little while and kept on working hard with no commitments. No bells going off. No sweet words whispered. And that was okay. That's what fit. Listening to you now, I realize we are both in the same place. We love each other dearly. We work well together. We understand each other and trust each other. I love you as my dearest friend, Lawrence. I wish you and Midge forever happiness. Now let's do what we do best together, and that is talk business."

"Thank you, Ivy. I am ready to talk business with you. I've missed our brainstorming sessions, but I have one request. Tell me more about your time away. I'm intrigued."

"Okay, here goes.

That began a lengthy conversation concerning her time back home. From her three special people to the yellow house to Izzie and Izzie's family, the Mitten Path, more and more about Walter and the cubbyholes, being reunited with her diary, her sketches, her very first desk, and that Picasso hidden away.

"That all happened within a week's time?"

"Those were some of the highlights. There's much more."

When their entrees were served, they were discussing Ivy's idea for the charity auction.

"We both know it has to be spectacular so we can bring in lots of money to give away. I told you about Elena. I told you about finding that first velvet green gown in a cubbyhole. Let's build a massive campaign around the gown. We'll tell the story, the whole story from my being ditched at the Holiday Ball to finding the dress in a cubbyhole, stressing it was my very first design. As Elena says, it is my original Picasso. The night of the open house, we'll have a model wearing it throughout the evening."

"I have an idea. Why not ask Elena to model it? She is part of the story."

"Brilliant, Lawrence. That's why I love you so. You are brilliant. I will call Elena and her father later to get their reaction. If they are on board, I'll get the gown cleaned and we'll hammer out a press release. I love it when the juices are flowing. We are such a great team."

They kept talking, from one course to the next. As they were savoring their tiramisu with coffee, Ivy had a few more brilliant ideas.

"While I was home, Andy, Doc's grandson, went with me on a tour of my old house on the lane thanks to an invitation from the present owners. Andy likened that to my tying up loose ends. I appreciate that term. I have a few loose ends I'd like to tie up with you, Lawrence."

Taking a sip of her coffee, Ivy elaborated. "The first loose end I am asking is for your input. Since I loved being back home, spending time in my farmhouse and cooking and relaxing, do you think we could keep up with everything that needs to be done if I were to move home? Trains run back and forth all the time. Of course I'd spend time here as well. Lots of time, and when in a pinch or on a deadline, I would be here. And I'd be here for events and such. We could hire someone to keep it organized, freeing you up to do what you do best—promote, double-check my work, pay the bills, and a thousand other things. The farmhouse is big enough for me to have an office, a studio, and a showroom. We could market it so it sounds intriguing because it will be. I'll have sheep and horses, maybe even a few reindeer on the property. And best of all, Lawrence, my sister is only three hours away. I'll be able to be an active part of her children's lives. Don't you think we need to reorganize? Not slow down, because we need to be competitive, but reinvent our time and our days and change the way we live. Keep our heads held high. Life goes by in a second. I don't want to miss one more thing."

"I totally support your idea as well as the thinking that went into it. For me, it was Midge who slowed me down, and now she will be my wife. Imagine that Ivy. I am getting married."

"Midge is very lucky. I have an offer to make you, Lawrence. I feel it is perfectly timed with what we are discussing as well as you getting married. I would like to make you my partner. That is another loose end, and I want to take care of it as soon as possible. We can work out the details. I know you will be pleased."

Raising his coffee cup, Lawrence accepted her offer. "A toast to my partner and to your extended location."

"I must add to our conversation this very important point. We must never take our focus off the quality we have become known for both in our designs and the material we use to turn those designs into gowns and various merchandise."

"I agree, Ivy. After what we've been through to reach this point, we can never skimp on quality. That's what our brand represents, along with creativeness and fine fabrics."

It was snowing when Ivy left the restaurant. Lawrence offered her a ride home, but she felt like walking—until she got further down the sidewalk and her feet in those heels were freezing. She was freezing. Ivy wished she was wearing her parka with the hood and her snow boots and talking to Hazel. Ivy couldn't wait to go doll shopping.

The moment she walked into her apartment, Ivy hurried up to the bedroom and changed into her pajamas. Then she went back downstairs to the kitchen. After pouring herself some juice, Ivy went into the living room and stood there. She couldn't figure out where to sit. While all the chairs and sofas were of the finest quality, tops of the top brand names, they weren't comfortable. She had to admit they'd never been comfortable. She'd grown to liking her old sofa in the farmhouse. Worn, yet so comfortable. After sitting on the floor wrapped in blankets searching the web for information on making someone a partner, her phone rang. She wasn't going to answer it, until she thought it might be Lawrence with even more ideas. They'd always joke how they felt drunk after one of their brainy sessions. Their heads would be spinning.

So up she got and answered the phone.

"Hello? Oh, hi, Andy. Something wrong with the reindeer?"

It turned out there was something wrong with Susan. While out to dinner, she told Andy there was no way she'd ever come back to him. That guy with the slick black hair asked her to marry him, and she'd accepted. "Susan told me the only reason she stopped at Doc's was to give him her gift and nothing else. She made a point of saying no one present in the kitchen that evening had any right to be involved. She ended by saying she's not looking back."

"I am so sorry, Andy."

"Strange isn't it? I thought after Susan considered what Grampa said, she'd understand why I did what I did. But in the end, she was right to want no part of me or our marriage."

"Why do you say that?"

"I've tried telling myself I still love her. But after everyone left Grampa's the other night, I walked down to the barn and spent some time with the reindeer. I thought about the big change they were facing. I was worried how they'd handle the move. Then I thought about everything Grampa said, and that's when it hit me, Ivy. If our marriage had been strong in the first place, we could have worked through the storms, but we didn't. I have no doubt the reindeer will be fine. They will work through adjusting to the change together. We never did that. Not once. And if we were to get back together knowing what we do now, it still wouldn't work. I can't put Elena through that again. It is over."

"How did Elena react?"

"She told me to get on with my life, and guess what, Ivy? I've decided to do just that."

"Wonderful. I'm happy for you, Andy. It's none of my business, but have you made any decisions as to what you might do?"

"I called to share with you some things I have decided. First, I'm going to move the office outside the village and bring in a partner so my time is more flexible. And here's the kicker, Ivy. Once I have a partner and things are back on track, I'll be playing the guitar with that band I played with the other night."

"Andy, I am so happy for you. Things will keep falling into place now that you've taken some giant steps forward."

"Thanks, Ivy. I miss you. Life around here is not the same without you."

"Watch out, Andy. I too am making some changes and if all falls into place, I'll be spending more time back home."

Sitting on the floor in her pajamas, Ivy told Andy about her conversation with Lawrence. When she got to the idea of having Elena model the Picasso, Andy was all for it.

"But that's up to Elena. Call her tomorrow after school. January in New York is getting more exciting by the day."

Ivy called Elena early the next morning before she went to school. Ivy couldn't wait all day to talk to her."

"I would love to model that original velvet gown, Ivy! Think it will fit me?"

"I'm taking it to the cleaners today and putting a rush on it. Then I will express it to Vivian. You can go to her shop and try it on. If it needs tweaking, she can do that right away. Then return it to me, and I'll take it back to the cleaners."

It turned out there was no problem with the dress. After Vivian made a few adjustments, Ivy had it back at the cleaners while she and Lawrence got busy on a massive promotion benefiting New York City charities.

Six days before Christmas, Ivy went toy shopping. It didn't take her long to make Hazel's wishes come true. Of course, Louise and Teddy would be happy as well.

As the sales lady wrapped Ivy's purchases in Christmas paper designed with little teddy bears in Santa hats, she wished Ivy a merry Christmas.

"Some little ones are going to be happy on Christmas morning. That's what Christmas is all about."

"I've never Christmas shopped for little ones. Now I can't wait until they open their gifts. Funny. I thought I outgrew getting excited like I did when I believed in Santa Claus."

"I'm a grandmother of five. The youngest is four. I was thinking the other day how lucky I am that she still believes because her excitement rubs off on me. Enjoy those little ones. They really do grow up too fast."

Walking out of the store onto West Thirty-Fourth, something in a window display of a nearby bookstore caught Ivy's attention. Minutes later she continued up the avenue with a few books on Picasso wrapped and in her shopping bag.

Christmas Eve came free of any commitments with those in the industry. Oh, there were parties, and she and Lawrence were invited, but they weren't going. Instead, Ivy was cooking on Christmas Eve. It would be a first. So was meeting Midge. She and Lawrence would be Ivy's guests. They arrived exactly at six with a bottle of wine and a gift certificate to Lawrence's family restaurant.

Ivy found Midge to be charming. Her short, dark, curly hair and pearly glasses complimented Lawrence's leather jacket and John Lennon rimmed glasses. His black patent leather shoes weren't the warmest things to wear.

"Your feet are going to freeze," Ivy remarked, when he came through the front door.

"I seem to recall you wearing heels not too long ago out in the snow."

"But I didn't have far to go, Lawrence."

"Oh, Ivy, you always win the war!"

"No comment, but I will say you two make a handsome couple. I am so happy to meet you, Midge."

"Thanks for asking us, Ivy. I've heard so much about you. Congratulations on all your success. You deserve it."

"I could not have achieved a thing without Lawrence. He keeps me organized, and I love how he's always coming through with ideas just when I've hit a brick wall."

"Lawrence is an amazing man. He makes me very happy."

They were sitting in the living room with the tree lights lit on a real Christmas tree and a fire in the fireplace and a window with the curtains pulled back overlooking Christmas Eve in New York City with all of its splendor when Ivy thanked them again for coming.

"Before we sit down to the very first prime rib dinner with all the trimmings that I've ever prepared, I would like to give you this, Lawrence. It is a small gift for always being by my side and for accepting my offer of becoming my partner."

Opening a small box wrapped in shimmering snowflake paper, Lawrence was overtaken by a personal check.

"Ivy. You do not have to do this. It is very kind, but I did not expect such an amount. Or any amount."

"It comes from my heart, Lawrence. I have one more gift, but it comes with strings attached. Please, open this now. I can't wait to explain what it represents."

Handing something square and beautifully wrapped to Lawrence, Ivy waited. When he held up a framed, childlike design, he looked puzzled. Ivy couldn't wait to explain her idea.

"I told you about my diary and the sketches I did when I was young and how I lost them when my parents divorced and we had to move. Well, all of that stuff was found in one of Doc's cubbyholes. I told you about the cubbyholes, right?"

"Yes, you did."

"I'm thinking of creating a line."

"Oh, here goes my partner again, Midge. When Ivy says that, she's already designing that new line of merchandise in her head."

"Those are creative juices at work, Lawrence."

"Thank you, Midge. That is exactly what's going on. I thought we'd call it "Designs from the Yellow House," but we'll have a brainstorming session before deciding. I'd update the scribbles and we'd launch the line a year from this coming spring. All the merchandise would be made in yellow material. Material of all kinds. Key is the story we'd craft. It would explain the house wasn't always yellow. It would tell about my parents divorcing. How we moved out of that place we called home. Our first home. It would include a photo of the desk my grandfather made now back in my possession. That's where I sat and did the scribbles. We'd include an image of the original scribble to give the item a sense of story. Let's get through January's event, then we'll talk. What do you think?"

"Absolutely love the idea, Ivy. It has such depth. So many would identify with what you went through. How you felt. So many would be interested in how you went from then to now. That part of your story needs to be told."

Her first Christmas Eve as chef was a major success in so many ways, including the dinner.

Ivy had planned to sleep in on Christmas morning, but her phone ringing a little before seven had her wide awake. As she went to answer it, Ivy thought of so many Christmas mornings, running down front stairs to see what Santa had brought her. When she answered the phone, a little girl with yellow braids bubbling over with excitement reminded Ivy of how she used to sound after opening her Christmas gifts.

"Thank you, Aunt Ivy, for my doll with lots of yellow hair. Her name is Sunny, and she is sleeping in her doll bed with her blankets!"

"Merry Christmas, Hazel! I think Sunny is a perfect name. I'm glad she is asleep in her bed. Did Santa eat his cookies you and Louise left out for him?"

"Yes, he did, and he drank his milk."

After talking with Izzie and thanking her for the beautiful family portrait, they started reminiscing about Christmas mornings in the yellow house when it wasn't yellow.

"Remember when Santa brought your play kitchen with the cupboards full of little plastic plates and cups and I started crying for my own kitchen?"

"I do remember that Christmas, Izzie. I felt so sad for you. That's why I proposed we make a deal, and it worked."

"It was a good deal. You let me play in your kitchen, and I let you play with my finger paints."

"That was the best deal I've ever made. I always wanted some finger paints. Probably even more than a pretend kitchen with plastic plates and cups."

"It was obvious, Ivy. You used most of the finger paints and all the paper that came with the paints. I didn't care. I played in your pretend kitchen with buttons on the stove that really moved."

"And Mom never said a thing because we both were having fun, meaning we were content."

The sisters said goodbye when Willie started fussing.

Ivy went to her studio for most of the day. She knew it would be quiet. And it was. Ivy was able to do a lot of catching up, even as thoughts of a little girl with a doll named Sunny came back around again and again.

Chapter Nineteen

FINALLY, AFTER HOURS OF PLANNING AND decorating and creating, it was almost time for the much anticipated event taking place on a January evening in the heart of New York City, where businesses and celebrities would be joining together to raise money for worthy charities. Those participating businesses would stay open late, offering reduced prices on several items with all revenue going to those in need. Original work by well-known artists, created exclusively for the event, would be auctioned off for the cause. Fashion icons, such as Ivy Nolan, would auction off an original of their choice.

There was great excitement up and down the streets of the city. Christmas lights remained up. The Rockettes would perform one exclusive show at Radio City Music Hall the night before the event. All proceeds would be donated. Musicians would be out at random locations playing holiday favorites. A massive fireworks extravaganza in Times Square would bring the event to an unforgettable close.

Ivy's guests checked into the Ritz-Carlton late in the afternoon, the day before it all began. For January, the weather was perfect. Ivy had arranged a horse-drawn carriage ride through Central Park for them as well as skating in Rockefeller Center, and tickets to the Rockettes. She made them dinner reservations and ordered welcome baskets for their rooms. Ivy and Lawrence were so busy that they never got to see them until a few hours before the event the following evening. That's when Doc and Vivian, Andy and Elena, and Murphy and his daughter, Angela, arrived at Ivy Nolan's showroom on Madison Avenue. Everyone hugged and thanked Ivy over and over again.

"We aren't staying, Ivy. We are on our way back to the hotel to get changed. We just wanted to say thank you. We are having a wonderful time."

"I am so glad you stopped in, Doc. Having you all with me tonight is more than I ever could have imagined happening."

"I love our hotel, Ivy. It is so luxurious. My bed is huge. And the carriage ride around Central Park was so much fun. I love New York!"

"I'm glad you're here, Elena. I've missed you."

Everyone loved Lawrence. He and Midge fit right in.

"Your showroom looks like a centerspread right out of *Vogue*, Ivy."

"Thank you, Vivian. Lawrence has a flair for decorating."

"Ivy! I love these designer jeans. I saw them on your website."

"Pick out a pair, Elena. There are tops and boots too."

"I wasn't aware you designed anything other than wedding gowns, Ivy."

"Well, the bride has to be dressed for her honeymoon as well, Andy."

"I see the lingerie, Ivy." Vivian smiled. "Simply beautiful."

"Pick out whatever you would like, Vivian. You are a bride-to-be. Have you and Doc decided on where you will go on your honeymoon?"

"Yes. We will be going home."

"I think that's perfect, Vivian. As I said, pick out whatever you'd like. Honeymooning at home could be lots of fun."

"Oh, you are the silly one." Vivian laughed as she studied the lingerie on the racks.

Noticing Murphy and his daughter looking at bridesmaids' dresses, Ivy went over to see if they had questions.

"If you see something you'd like, it is yours, Angela. The showroom is open to both you and your wedding party. Your dad told me you purchased one of my wedding gowns. Thanks so much. You will be a most beautiful bride."

"Thank you, Ivy, and thanks for your generous offer. Mom thought you'd be busy enough, so we decided we'll go to your website and then we'll be in touch."

"You can always come back another time. It's hard to pick dresses out online. I tell most everyone how feeling the fabric is as important as seeing the dress. Fabric makes such a difference."

"I couldn't have said it any better than that, Ivy."

"I probably heard you say that more than once, Vivian."

Time was flying by. Excitement was building. Everyone but Elena returned to the hotel to get dressed for the evening.

As Ivy led Elena upstairs, the young woman explained her mother didn't come because she felt out of place. "But she's coming when the Elena Collection debuts."

"She's welcome anytime, Elena."

Walking down a narrow hallway, Ivy stopped in front of a grand window overlooking Madison Avenue. The view was breathtaking. Standing next to Ivy, Elena asked Ivy if she ever got scared.

"Everyone gets scared."

"You get scared?"

"I do, Elena."

"I'd get scared too, if I lived here."

"Living here doesn't scare me anymore. I get scared if I can't come up with new designs or ideas right away. I worry I might run out of them."

"That could never happen."

"Why do you think that, Elena?"

"It's simple. Walter believes in you, and so do I."

They stood in front of the window for a few more minutes. Then they hurried to get dressed and back downstairs before Lawrence unlocked the door.

The original Winter Gown was on a hanger in a wardrobe in a room with a full-length mirror and a closet with odds and ends of gowns and dresses.

"They're all samples. It sometimes takes a few tries to get what you are after," Ivy explained.

Escorting Elena into a dressing room, Ivy pointed out a pink, light-weight bathrobe, folded inside a plastic bag sitting on a chair.

"Put that on, Elena. My makeup girl will be in"

"A real makeup person! How exciting, Ivy!"

By ten past seven, Elena and Ivy were walking back down the hall-way, then down the stairs. A photographer followed them.

"You'll get used to Marcus. Try to ignore him. His job is to take photos. Ironically, we'll end up using just a few of them."

Reaching the door leading into the showroom, Ivy stopped with her hand on the knob.

"You look striking in that green velvet dress, Elena. I wouldn't want anyone but you to be wearing it. Smile. Hold your head high and enjoy the moment. Deep breath. Here we go."

Lawrence was hustling about, but he stopped when they stepped through the doorway.

"Twenty minutes to show time, ladies. You're both smashing. Gorgeous. Classic New York. Madison Avenue will never be the same. Oh, the money that is about to be raised."

Ivy looked fabulous in a cream silk velvet jumpsuit she'd designed especially for the evening. Under Lawrence's guidance, the showroom was enchanting with several real Christmas trees strung with tiny twinkling lights, festive décor, as well as a string quartet and champagne served in fine crystal glasses. Turnout was instant, as was the media coverage. Other revered designers took the time to stop by. Ivy introduced Elena to all of them. Most asked about the green velvet gown she was wearing, and some were interested in learning more about Elena's plans after graduation. Even a few gave her their business cards.

"We will be introducing that gown shortly," Ivy explained, as Doc and company returned.

"You all clean up beautifully. I love your red satin bow tie, Doc. It's the perfect touch with your beard. And Vivian, red is your color. Especially red satin. Did you make your dress and Doc's bowtie? Both are quite lovely."

"I did make them, Ivy. It felt wonderful to be sewing again.

"You are stunning, Ivy," said Andy. "You complement your surroundings."

"Thank you, Andy. Don't tell anyone, but I'd prefer to be back in the country."

"Really?"

"Really, Andy."

Elena approached her father. "Hi, Dad!"

"Oh, Elena. You look so beautiful."

"Thanks, Dad, but it's the makeup!"

"It's not the makeup, honey."

"Excuse me for now," said Ivy. "I have to mingle. It's just what one must do."

"You do it well."

"And you, Andy, clean up very nicely. Come with me, Elena. I'll teach you how to mingle New York style."

Andy enjoyed talking with guests as the showroom filled with all kinds of people. Ivy was introducing Elena to a few modeling agents when someone tapped her on the shoulder. Turning, Ivy was overjoyed to find Izzie standing there.

The sisters hugged without saying a word. Tears and laughter followed.

"Thank you so much for coming, Izzie."

"I can't imagine not being here to support you."

"You are a knockout in that brocade dress, Izzie. That's one of my favorites. The slight slit on the side adds a bit of fun to it."

"I love this dress. It is my very own Ivy Nolan Design. Teddy bought it for me as a Christmas gift."

"You enhance the dress, Izzie. You really do."

Calling Marcus over, Ivy asked that he take photos of Izzie in the brocade dress.

"I think I'll do a feature centered around brocade on the website. With your permission, Izzie, I'd like to include some of the photos of you."

"I'm thrilled, Ivy. Use whatever you like, keeping in mind I am not a model."

"I'll send you some of the photos once I have them and we can talk. I forgot to ask. Did Teddy and the kids come, too?"

"No. Teddy thought I'd have a better time if the kids stayed home, so he is watching them while I'm here with you."

"What a thoughtful husband. I'll be sure to thank him."

"Mom and Dad thought about coming but hesitated only because they didn't want to embarrass you."

"They could never embarrass me, Izzie."

"I think they were more concerned about the scene they might create when first seeing you after all these years. While they can't wait to make that happen, they feel the moment should be personal. Mom cried like a baby when I told her about the Mitten Path and you meeting the kids."

"I understand where they are coming from. Maybe when I get back home more often, I can have everyone for dinner. They will be shocked to learn I'm cooking."

"That's a wonderful idea, Ivy. I'm so happy my kids will have all of you in their lives."

"I am the lucky one. I can't wait to become the aunt I want to be."

After Ivy introduced Izzie to Lawrence, who was flying by, and Izzie seemed comfortable with Doc and Vivian, Ivy went back to mingling. Looking about the studio, she noted Elena mingling with professional models her age.

She's a pro already. Connecting with young professional models as if they are best friends.

More and more people came. Magazine editors and TV producers as well as more revered designers and bigwigs, politicians, and the general public filled Ivy Nolan's studio.

On her way to welcome fellow designers, an odor came drifting by. It caught Ivy's attention. It made her stomach turn—again. The odor was coming from behind her. Turning, she found herself face to face with John—that John—who she'd last seen hurrying out the front door of the historic hotel in the downtown of her hometown. Ivy stood still, staring at him, just about gagging on his English Leather.

So many thoughts went through her head as he stood there smiling that obnoxious smile, seemingly expecting her to jump for joy that he'd returned. But he'd changed. Physically that is. Aging had not been kind to John. A potbelly was obvious, as was his lack of hair. He seemed shorter, which surprised Ivy when remembering the moment they'd met in celebration of his Ivy League school's football team winning a game on a Saturday afternoon in October. He seemed so tall way back then and sure of himself, and when he held her in that moment, Ivy nuzzled herself against his fine woolen sweater, feeling safe and warm and happy and certain she was in love with this stranger who had a dimple on his chin and a smile that let her know he wanted to make love to her, forever. But here they were, some twenty years later, and that dimple looked like a crater on his very big chin. Despite his many changes, that smirk of a smile and his aftershave gave him away. When he went to hug her, Ivy moved aside.

"It's been too long, Ivy. I'm back in the city on business. I read about your gig and thought I'd take you out for a drink when it's over. We can catch up, if you know what I mean."

"Where's Linda?"

"That didn't last long. As soon as the baby was born, we split. So, what do you say about getting together later?"

In a whisper, John added, "We have some unfinished business to take care of, if you know what I mean."

"Can you wait a minute, John? I have some business of my own to take care of right now."

"Looking good, Ivy. Looking good. I'm ready to make up for lost time."

Despite thinking she might get sick, Ivy found Elena. Standing in front of the quartet, Ivy quieted everyone down. Then she welcomed them and introduced Elena. Then Ivy told a story.

"Most of you know Lawrence. He is the reason I'm able to do what I love to do. Lawrence takes care of everything else. And soon, he will become my partner as I relocate a share of this operation to my hometown, to my farmhouse that will become a division of Ivy Nolan Designs. This Madison Avenue location will remain open. Nothing will change our way of operating. Before I continue, I'd like Lawrence to come up here with his lovely fiancée, Midge."

Seconds later, the couple was standing next to Ivy. Everyone applauded. Everyone was aware Lawrence was the force behind top designer Ivy Nolan. Although the many successful designers present were competitors, they were also a close-knit group.

"With the goal being to raise money tonight for those in need, I thought good and hard about what we could auction off. Recently I went home to visit three people who helped me tremendously along the way. Without them, I would not be standing here. One asked me to help him clean out his barn. In the process we found something very special to me."

Motioning for Elena to step out where everyone could see her, Ivy continued. "This gown is what we found, wrapped in tissue paper and stuffed into a cubbyhole. This was the first gown I designed. I was twenty years old. I had no clue what I was doing. All I knew was I wanted a gown that no one else would have because I'd been invited to a holiday ball at a fancy hotel in my hometown. To get that original gown, I went to a fabric shop where I met a talented seamstress. She taught me many things and showed me different types of fabric. When she showed me a bolt of velvet, I knew I wanted a velvet gown. I worked on the design. Then the seamstress took over. The result was this stunning gown. I was in my sophomore year at a community college. My date went to a nearby private school not far from mine. He was from New York. I'd never been to New York. Long story short, the night was a disaster. I ended up throwing this green velvet gown in the trash. Finding it in that cubbyhole was a miracle. Tonight I will be auctioning it off. I will include a notarized document with my signature stating the above.

"The gown is being modeled by Elena."

Everyone welcomed Elena with a round of applause. Then Ivy continued.

"I would like to introduce you to my three special friends, Doc, Vivan and Murphy. Three special friends, will you please stand up when I call out your name??

"Doc played a pivotal role in my life as I was growing up. My family and I lived next door. He is a veterinarian and a very good checkers player. It was in his barn full of reindeer that we found the velvet gown.

"Vivian is the seamstress who sewed the velvet gown. I spent lots of time in her fabric shop, where we not only worked with fabric, but we talked about using one's imagination.

"Murphy was the manager of that downtown hotel. He came to my rescue after my date left me. I ran upstairs to what was our room. I threw myself on the bed with that gown still on and fell asleep. When I woke up around two o'clock in the morning, I tossed the gown in the trash, got dressed, and ran downstairs and out the door. Murphy found me sitting outside in the cold, on a swing on the front porch of the hotel, not knowing what to do. He encouraged me to go back inside. He sat with me, and we talked. When I was ready, he drove me home.

"There's one more person I need to recognize. Andy, please step forward. Andy played in the band that night. He also did odd jobs around the hotel. That night his job was to empty the wastebaskets. He found my gown. Lucky for me he realized it was too good to throw out. He decided to take it to Doc's barn. Doc is his grandfather. But Doc was busy, so Andy wrapped the gown up and stuck it in a cubbyhole and there it sat until we recently found it.

"My first design is now up for the highest bid. Bidding will continue for the next two hours. All money raised will go to charity."

The studio was buzzing with excitement. Bidding was hot and competitive. After thanking the three who meant so much to her, Ivy went back to where John was waiting.

Making no reference to the story Ivy just told, John was anxious to get going.

"Ready?"

"Ready for what?"

"I have a room at the Plaza."

"And ..."

"And remember, we have some unfinished business?"

"I didn't have time earlier to tell you, but our business is finished."

"Aww, come on, Ivy. You know what I mean. Remember? The

champagne, the bed? Let's go pick up where we left off. You know you wanted me. Come on. Let's go."

"*Wanted* is in the past tense. It's behind us. Water under the bridge."

Taking hold of Ivy's arm, John insisted she go with him. "I like a girl who plays coy. Come on, Ivy. Time to go."

Andy stepped in. "Ivy's going nowhere, but you are."

"Ivy, tell your strong-arm to let go of me."

"Leave now, John. You've been water under the bridge for years now."

"You really are missing out on a good time."

"I'm having a good time, and by the way, I don't consider my business to be a gig. It is a commitment. Something you don't understand."

Without saying a word, John turned and walked out the door, his English Leather left floating in the air.

"You okay, Ivy?"

"I've never felt better. John was just another loose end."

The evening turned out to be one to remember. Monies raised went beyond expectations, setting a record. The auctioning off of the original winter gown had a lot to do with it. An unassuming woman wearing a simple gray suit, probably in her late forties with her almost-black hair pulled back in a French twist and only a touch of lipstick, made the winning bid. As she was taking care of the paperwork, Ivy was answering wedding gown questions asked by a young woman getting married in November.

"Excuse me, Ivy. You have a call."

"Thank you, Lawrence," Ivy replied, excusing herself for a moment.

Once in her office, Lawrence explained there was no phone call.

"I'll only take a minute, Ivy. I needed to tell you that the woman who bought the velvet gown is E. Jones, the Pulitzer Prize–winning journalist at the *Times*."

"You have to be kidding. That really is E. Jones?"

"It really is. I met her a few years ago at my parents' restaurant. She was sitting alone. Rumor has it E. Jones is a very private person. I am surprised she is here tonight. She could have sent someone to do her bidding."

"I think I will introduce myself and thank her for purchasing the gown. I wonder why she wanted it in the first place."

After going back and answering some other questions the engaged young woman had, Ivy went and introduced herself to E. Jones. Thanking her for her bid, Ivy asked why she was interested in the gown.

With a bit of a smile, E. Jones took hold of the gown. Her eyes seemed to study Ivy as she replied, "Every year since this annual event has been held, I've selected a few of the participating businesses from the many participating to go to and make a contribution. As I always do, I read the stories published in the *Times* about the participants. Your story stood out to me this time. Let me explain."

E. Jones was interrupted by a fan. A few minutes later, she continued. "As I was saying, your story stood out to me because my story is similar. May I call you Ivy?"

"Most definitely."

"I too had the support of certain adults as I was growing up. One was my high school English teacher, who would encourage me to keep writing. The other was a woman down the street from where I grew up. Without those two people supporting my ambition of becoming a journalist at the *Times*, I'd still be on that street, wishing I could be that person I wanted to be. When I think of it now, I laugh. I was intrigued by the *Times* from an early age. No other newspaper would do, and now it is such a part of my life. We have a lot in common, Ivy. I came tonight to support you and celebrate your success. In doing so, I would like to give you back your gown. It belongs with you. It is my gift to another taking care of what you described as loose ends."

"Your kindness and generosity are deeply appreciated. If ever I can repay you, please call me or stop by."

"I will be calling. I think we need to go out to dinner and talk some more. Best of luck with the move back to that farmhouse, Ivy. I think it is a wonderful idea. One more thing, I'm thrilled you have your desk back. It is such a part of your story. So glad we've met."

E. Jones hurried out the door.

Lawrence hurried to Ivy's side.

"She gave you back the dress! Unbelievable, Ivy. This has been one amazing night. I think we should top if off with fireworks in Times Square."

Doc spoke up. "We don't like to be party poopers, but we have to get to the airport early in the morning, and it takes us a little while to get moving."

Giving Ivy a hug, he continued. "We had a wonderful time. It was well worth dressing up in my favorite bow tie. I'm so happy for you, Ivy, and cannot wait to have you back home more often. And again, thank you for taking in my reindeer."

"Taking in your reindeer was the least I could do, Doc. There's really nothing I could do to ever repay you for your kindness."

Thanking Vivian for coming, Ivy invited her back. "I want to take you to the Garment District and spend as much time there as you would like. We can surround ourselves with bolts upon bolts of fabric."

"That would be a dream come true! Some spend their vacations on beaches. I'd much prefer spending time in the Garment District with you, Ivy."

Before Vivian and Doc went back to the hotel with Murphy and his daughter, Ivy gave Elena a gift for modeling the original winter gown. Pulling the box out of a bag, Elena was thrilled when she opened it and found a precious snow globe.

"I love it, Ivy. Oh, there's a rabbit with a reindeer. Thank you. I had so much fun."

"You make a beautiful model, Elena."

"Your gown made that easy. I have some new friends, Ivy, some modeling friends. We're going to keep in touch."

"I'm so glad. You can always stay with me when you come to New York. That is, if I'm not up north in my farmhouse!"

After things were wrapped up, Ivy, Andy, and Elena, along with Lawrence and Midge, went out on the town. Izzie was going with them, but it was late and her flight was early, just like Doc's.

"Next time I see you, we'll be back home. Thank you, Izzie, for coming."

"I had a wonderful time, Ivy. I'm so lucky to have you as my big sister. Who else could have made up a place called the Mitten Path? That would be you, only you, Ivy. Love you."

The fireworks were breathtaking. The crowd was gigantic. Just before the grand finale, it started snowing a little harder. Everyone broke out singing Christmas songs in the month of January. Elena was falling in love with New York City.

"Where to now?" Andy asked, when the show was over.

"There's a stage up in Central Park open to the public. No charge. Bands are playing until three, and beer tents are set up as well. Midge and I would love it if you all joined us."

"I want to go, Dad! Please! Let's go. We don't have to stay long. I know we're going back tomorrow."

"You've talked me into it, Elena. "What do you think, Ivy?"

"I think we need to flag down a cab and join the party!"

Central Park was mobbed with partiers. Some famous bands made appearances. Music was nonstop, like the snowflakes. No one was cold. Dancing took care of that. Around two, Ivy decided it was time for them to go.

Chapter Twenty

It turned out to be a busy year. Everyone was on the go. Doc moved into his new home. Andy relocated not too far out of the village in a stone home sitting along the river's edge. Elena graduated in June. Despite modeling agencies calling and a few of the models she'd met in New York visiting her, Elena remained clueless as to what she wanted to do for the rest of her life. While deciding, she was taking some basic online courses and staying at her father's new place. Elena loved having her bedroom window overlooking the river. The property came with a few outbuildings. One was big enough for Andy's office. Contractors added on kennels and a parking area. Dr. Andy Armstrong opened his practice in early April.

Ivy's attempt to divide her time between the farmhouse and the city was harder to implement than she'd imagined. After January's charity event and the great time she'd had twisting the night away with Elena, and Andy getting up on stage when asked to play the guitar and Lawrence and Midge winning a dance contest, she told Elena and Andy to keep in touch. But once everyone got back into a routine, they all picked up where they'd left off.

Ivy missed Elena's graduation due to an industry event in Paris. She'd missed Andy's grand opening and Hazel's birthday. When Vivian called a week before Thanksgiving to ask Ivy a question, Ivy put the brakes on.

"Good morning, Ivy. I thought I'd catch you before your day begins."

"It is so nice to hear your voice, Vivian. How are you and Doc doing with that beautiful home? I understand the reindeer love their new surroundings."

"The reindeer are quite content, although Walter seemed lost for a while. Doc is like a new man, Ivy. It's as if he's left the ghosts of his past on that lane and started over."

"I'm sure that's exactly what he's done, Vivian. Have you moved in completely?"

"Call me old-fashioned, but I'm not moving in until we are married. That doesn't mean I'm not here when I'm out of work because I am. I love every minute we are together. That's what I wanted to talk to you about. Do you have a few minutes, Ivy?"

"I have as much time as you need, Vivian."

"Doc and I have an idea and we would like your honest input."

"I'm listening."

"With everyone moving around and Elena's graduation and now the holidays approaching, we've had such a hard time figuring out when we'd gather together those we love for our wedding."

"It has been extra busy, I agree. How many people were you thinking of inviting?"

"Not many. Just our immediate family and your family as well, maybe Murphy's."

"What do you have in mind?"

"Between the two of us, we have everything we need. We'd prefer the wedding to be a celebration."

"That makes sense."

"We would like to invite everyone for a Christmas Eve dinner with all the trimmings and excitement one would expect. Once the dinner has been enjoyed, we'd like to surprise our guests by getting married right then and there. No gifts. No wedding fanfare. We'd like it to be both simple and simply beautiful. Do you think that would work, seeing that it is Christmas Eve?"

"So, no one would know until the moment?"

"Correct. Andy and Elena would be standing up for us, and they'll already be there, so we can surprise them too."

"I love your idea. I couldn't think of anything more romantic than to be married on Christmas Eve. I have one suggestion, Vivian."

"That's why we decided to tell you and only you, Ivy. What is your suggestion?"

"If you agree, my gift to you and Doc would be my home with all the trimmings for your Christmas Eve wedding. You can be married in my home, and I will take care of every single detail, including the expense. However you'd like me to decorate, I will do it. We'll never let on there's a wedding. I'll invite them to a Christmas Eve dinner and when they leave, they will be taking with them memories they will never forget. And you and Doc can go back to a home minus the mess and the pickup."

"We can't let you take care of every single detail, Ivy. I know Doc will not allow you to pay for everything."

"He will have no choice if you accept my gift. Tell him if you come by reindeer and sleigh, he can pay for any more hay that might be needed."

"I will talk your generous offer over with Doc. Wherever we celebrate, I would appreciate your creative input, making it as beautiful an evening as possible."

"Of course, I will help. We can brainstorm once I finally get back there, which will be very soon."

"Andy tells us how busy you are, Ivy. I don't know how you do what you do."

"I've said it before. I couldn't do what I do without Lawrence."

"Are you coming home for Thanksgiving?"

"No. Since I won that award last year, I am expected to be at this year's event in early December to present the award to this year's recipient. There are lots of details to take care of before that happens. But we can do some Zoom meetings, and I'll take care of everything. I will be there no later than the tenth."

"That is plenty of time. One more thing, Ivy, and then I'll let you go. Would you consider wearing that original velvet gown on Christmas Eve?"

"After fitting it to Elena, I'm sure it would never fit me."

"Send it to me along with your measurements and I'll make it work. You and Elena are close in size."

"That made my day. Elena calls that gown my original Picasso. I'd love to wear it to your wedding, my dear friend."

After picking a date and time for a Zoom call, they hung up.

Chapter Twenty-One

Ivy HAD BEEN HOME ABOUT A week when it happened.

She'd been so preoccupied by ordering trees and wreaths and flowers as well as gifts that were wrapped and delivered to her doorstep and moving furniture and getting help to clean and finding a chef to take over the Christmas Eve dinner that would include a magnificent cake and prime rib with all the trimmings and fabulous hors d'oeuvres and getting up the nerve to call her parents and invite them for Christmas Eve that she'd blocked out any conversations not related to the Christmas Eve wedding event she was working on. Oh, she thought she heard what others were saying. She acted like she did. But it became obvious after the accident that she hadn't heard one word of what Doc and Andy and Elena were saying about Walter.

They were worried. The mighty reindeer wasn't eating. He wasn't happy in his new surroundings. Whenever he could, Walter would take off and show up at Ivy's. He missed Pearl. During his stay in Ivy's barn, he'd spend afternoons resting by Pearl. He'd gotten used to the barn, making one particular area with a window all his own.

A few nights before Christmas Eve, Ivy received a call from the state police.

"Ivy. This is Sergeant Daniel Addison from the state police. We went to school together. I've been told you house reindeer in your barn at times. Is that true?"

"I remember you in my biology class, Dan. To answer your question, yes, I sometimes house reindeer in my barn. Why do you ask?"

"One of my officers came upon a pretty big reindeer lying at the end of your driveway. I think he was hit. He isn't moving."

"I'm on my way."

Grabbing her phone and a blanket, Ivy ran out the door. On her way, she called Andy in tears.

"I'll pick Doc up and we'll be right there, Ivy. Talk softly to him. Walter knows your voice."

Ivy did what Andy suggested. Sergeant Addison and a few more troopers were able to move Walter further off the road. All the while, Ivy kept whispering to him.

"You are going to be fine, Walter. Don't worry. Doc and Andy will be here any minute. Don't worry. Santa is coming. Christmas is near, Walter."

When Andy and Doc arrived, Ivy didn't say a word. She stepped aside and let the doctors take over. A few seconds later, one of the side doors of Andy's truck opened. It was Elena. Shaking and crying. Taking her into her arms, Ivy consoled the young woman.

"He opened his eyes when I talked to him, Elena. He is in good hands. Say some prayers. They will be heard."

"Are you sure? Why did this happen in the first place? Walter never hurt anything or anyone."

"Things don't make sense sometimes. But that shouldn't stop us from praying."

With all the lights and police cars, vehicles passing by slowed down to see what was going on. When an overloaded truck was trying to get by, he honked his horn to get people to move out of the way. That horn frightened Walter. He lifted his head and looked around.

"That's a good sign, Grampa. I can't find anything broken. We can do some radiographs and make sure."

Just then, Elena came over, knelt down, and hugged Walter. The reindeer reacted. He tried getting up. With Elena's help, he did. He stood straight up.

"Well, look at that. You're better than a pill, Elena."

"Is Walter okay, Gramps?"

"I think so. Something must have spooked him. Maybe a car. A truck. Whatever it was, he lost his footing and fell hard onto the pavement and was most likely knocked out for a minute. What do you think, Andy?"

"I agree. I do think we need to figure out how we make Walter comfortable when he's in your barn, Grampa, or this will keep happening."

Ivy spoke up. "While you figure that out, Walter is welcome to say here."

Giving Ivy a hug, Andy thanked her. So did Doc. Elena had a suggestion.

"I want to stay the night with Walter. His problem is, he's lonely. He loved Pearl and Pearl loved him back. If we figure out how to make him feel he is loved and not alone, Walter will be content in your barn, Gramps."

The two veterinarians looked at each other.

"Your diagnosis is correct, Elena. No one, not even a mighty reindeer, likes to be lonely," Doc remarked.

With patience, Walter made it to Ivy's barn. Elena and Andy made him a bed in the hay. Ivy filled a trough with fresh, cold water.

"I can make a bed upstairs for you, Elena. The hayloft would be warmer than down here."

"Thanks, Ivy, but I think I'll sleep out here with Walter. I'll only need blankets and a pillow. Dad, could you pick me up early in the morning? I have to do some shopping, then come back and see Walter before I go home."

"Whatever you want, Elena. I'll be here first thing in the morning. You can take me to my office and keep the car to do what you have to do."

The plan made sense.

After everyone left, Elena settled down near Walter. About midnight, Ivy brought her a cup of hot chocolate.

Elena was wide awake and quite warm and cozy.

"Thanks, Ivy. This reminds me of the story you told about you and Murphy having a cup of hot chocolate after that creep left you at the hotel."

"This cup of hot chocolate is in celebration of Walter not being injured."

"Cheers, Ivy." Elena smiled, holding up her cup.

"Cheers to you and Walter. If you need anything, there's an intercom inside that cupboard."

"We will be fine. I like making animals happy."

"You do that very well. Have a good sleep, Elena."

As Ivy was opening the door, Elena stopped her. "You make really good hot chocolate."

"That makes me happy. Night, Elena."

Chapter Twenty-Two

IT SNOWED A LITTLE MORE OVERNIGHT. While Elena waited for her father, she took Walter down under the trees to say good morning to Pearl. The reindeer was moving a little slow.

"You scared me last night. Please be careful. I know what sadness feels like, Walter. It will go away. You won't always feel like crying."

Kneeling down by Pearl, Elena cleared away the snow covering up stray leaves and twigs. Walter stood close by. Hearing a vehicle coming down the driveway, Elena stood. But it wasn't her father. A UPS truck was making its way to the farmhouse with another delivery. Tomorrow was Christmas Eve, and Ivy had lots to get in place. Opening the front door, Ivy signed for the merchandise. Then she put her coat and toque on and joined Elena and Walter.

"Would you like something to eat or drink, Elena?"

"No thanks, Ivy. Dad should be here any minute. Are you ready for Christmas Eve? Do you need some help?"

"To be honest, I've hired a chef, some cleaners, movers, and decorators to help me. I want tomorrow night to be magical. I think I've told you I haven't seen my parents in quite some time. Years, in fact. They'll be here and I'm feeling like a nervous kid. I'm afraid what to say or ask."

"You're afraid, just like Walter. I told him he won't always feel like crying."

Looking at the young woman, Ivy thanked her. "Your words are just what I needed to hear. I'll be wearing my Picasso. Vivian altered the gown again and somehow it fits me."

"I can't wait, Ivy. I love Christmas Eve. It's most always full of surprises."

"I agree," Ivy replied, thinking about the red cutter and the little reindeer as well as Doc and Vivian about to say their wedding vows.

"I hear Dad's car. He thinks he's cool in his Mustang."

"Your father is very cool. So are you."

Getting out of his car, Andy told Elena to shut her eyes.

"Don't look."

"Come on, Dad! It's not Christmas yet."

"It will feel like Christmas to one particular reindeer."

"Dad!"

"Put your arms out straight."

Elena did as her father asked.

"There you go. Merry Christmas to you and Walter."

Ivy could tell what was in the box. Tears fell from her eyes as Elena let out a subdued shout for joy. She didn't want to scare Walter.

"Dad! Where did you get this bunny? She looks just like Pearl."

"I still have an open line to Santa Claus. He told me to bring the bunny in the house tonight. Tomorrow you can introduce her to the barn."

"Can I introduce her to Walter?"

"Walter's introducing himself."

If ever there was a perfect Christmas present for a tired old reindeer, the bunny in the cardboard box was it. Walter was like a little kid coming down the front stairs on a Christmas morning and seeing the present of a lifetime under the tree with his name on it.

"Dad, Walter is happy again."

"Merry Christmas, Elena."

A rumbling coming down the driveway attracted everyone's attention.

Andy explained. "Grampa thought we should get Walter back to his barn sooner than later. The longer he stays here, the harder it will be to get him to leave. With Grampa's hauler out of commission, we've hired this hauler to do the job. I'm hoping having the bunny will help him make the adjustment."

"Good idea, Dad. I'll still need your car. I have some shopping to do."

Ivy's day was a busy one.

By the time she went to bed, everything was in place. The original Winter Gown was hanging in her closet. The weather forecast included snow. Most important, Walter was content.

Everything was in place for a Christmas Eve full of surprises.

Chapter Twenty-Three

A DREAM WOKE IVY UP AROUND two thirty. It'd been one of those dreams that seemed so real that she stayed still and tried to figure it out. Ivy was certain she could smell those sour cream chocolate chip cookies baking. Baking somewhere. At least in her dream she could. Probably because it was Christmas Eve, and for every Christmas Eve growing up, there would be freshly baked sour cream chocolate chip cookies to eat. Everyone loved them. So much so that over the years her grandmother and then her mother until the divorce would bake a big batch of the cookies very early on Christmas Eve morning. No matter which one was doing the baking, they'd put some of the cookies out to be enjoyed on a family heirloom glass plate. It was a vintage plate embossed with a sleigh and reindeer. When the plate was close to being empty, they'd put more cookies out. And when everyone was leaving, they'd each receive a small brown bag full of those delicious cookies. When going home from their grandmother's on Christmas Eve, Ivy and Izzie ate the cookies. Lots of sour cream chocolate chip cookies.

Thinking about that plate, Ivy jumped out of bed and ran down to the kitchen. She went searching through the cupboards, certain she'd find the plate. But she didn't. Standing in front of the bay window, Ivy relaxed right there in the middle of the night by doing one of her favorite things she used to do when she and Izzie were little and living in the yellow house. Back then, the sisters would sometimes sit on Ivy's bed when the snow was coming down and watch snowflakes fall.

"Pick a snowflake, Izzie. See if you can watch it fall all the way to the ground."

"I can't do that, Ivy!"

"Yes, you can. Watch me. It's easy."

Ivy made it look easy. She always succeeded in watching a snowflake hit the ground. At least that's what she'd tell Izzie.

"Did you see that? I watched another one all the way down."

Watching snowflakes kept them sitting on Ivy's bed for a very long time. Sometimes they'd take a break and start tickling each other. They'd laugh so hard that their mother would call up the backstairs to stop.

Ivy couldn't remember seeing one snowflake hit the ground. She never told Izzie.

Staying still, the image of the snow globe she'd found in a closet came to mind. The closet was in the small apartment her mother moved Izzie and Ivy to after divorcing.

"That's where I saw that plate. It was in a pillowcase with the snow-globe."

Ivy hurried to the pantry. She grabbed hold of a pillowcase sitting on a shelf.

Back in the kitchen, she pulled that vintage plate out. It was in perfect shape. She gave it a good washing. Dried it and set it on the counter. Checking the time, she decided to make a batch of those cookies. But she'd have to hurry. Santa's helpers would be arriving early.

Bags! I need some brown paper bags. Small ones.

Ivy texted the chef. She told him what she was doing, told him she needed those brown bags. He replied immediately, telling Ivy he'd be glad to pick some up. He told her not to worry about doing the cleaning up. He'd have one of his assistants do it.

Pulling the handwritten recipe out of the only cookbook she owned, Ivy gathered the ingredients and got busy. Lighting a candle as the snow whispered by the window, Ivy was certain she could hear the string of bells adorning precious little Scarlett, the reindeer Doc was caring for that Christmas Eve out in the barn on the lane. The wonder of the season was everywhere, even in the oven as that aroma came drifting by.

The caterer was first to arrive, followed by the florist and the guy from the liquor store. The tree decorator stopped to make sure there were no problems with any of the real trees he'd put up and decorated. By noon, Ivy's list was getting smaller, but the phone kept ringing. When Andy called around one o'clock, Ivy was getting nervous. In a few more hours, her parents would be arriving with Izzie and family.

"What time do you think you'll get here?"

"If all goes well, I should be there no later than three thirty. Elena can't wait. Grampa and Vivian told me earlier they want to go by reindeer and sleigh. Guess I can't stop them."

"I think that's romantic. Don't worry about them."

By two thirty the gifts Ivy had purchased for Izzie's little ones were under the tree. The table was set. The string quartet was in place. Ivy looked stunning in her Picasso. The caterer, baker, bartender, and chef all complimented Ivy on how beautiful she looked in that original velvet gown. Just as she was feeling blessed and confident, the doorbell rang. Her heart took off.

With a deep breath and one last look around, Ivy cleared her throat and went to the door to welcome her family back in her life. Turns out, it was an easy thing to do.

No one but Hazel was able to talk. Tears flowed as the snowflakes fell. When able, Ivy greeted her parents like they'd never been apart. She tried not making much of her father being in a wheelchair.

"What a beautiful home, Ivy. Congratulations on your great success."

"Thanks, Dad. You're looking well. I've missed you."

"I've missed you too, Ivy."

Father and daughter embraced. Despite her father being weak, to Ivy he was a tower of strength. After all, he was her father. Regardless of the turmoil they'd been through, the good times were the memories that came to mind. As her father spoke, with Christmas lights behind him and Christmas music playing, Ivy thought of the Christmases living on the lane. What a journey it had been.

"I had a health scare, but I'm listening to the doctors now and feeling better. Some days I still need the wheelchair. This seems to be one of them. Your mom has been a big help."

"I try to tell your father, Ivy, that just because we're divorced, it doesn't mean we don't care, because we do."

Ivy noticed her mother taking her father's hand. She felt like a little girl, happy because her parents seemed happy. Time made sense of some things that had torn her to pieces when she was a little girl, wanting her family back together while not understanding a thing about relationships. All she wanted was the four of them to be happy, and now, Ivy understood. They were happy as life continued on.

"Mom! Izzie told me about your website. How wonderful for you. I'm spreading the word on social media."

"Thank you, sweetheart. I can't imagine accomplishing all that you have. We are so proud of you."

"It all started on the lane, Mom. I'm so thankful we grew up where we did."

"I'm sorry I had to sell that house."

"I want you and Dad to understand I realize you did the best you could. I know you loved us. Now here we are together. You're grandparents and I'm an aunt."

Izzie and Teddy, holding Willie, joined them.

"Your home looks absolutely gorgeous, Ivy."

"Thanks, Izzie. I had lots of help. How's the hotel?"

"Very nice. Thanks for inviting us to stay with you, but the kids can get wild. That room full of toys you've fixed for the girls out on your sunporch is a good idea. Let's hope they don't want to eat in there."

The doorbell rang again. This time it was Andy and Elena, followed by Murphy and his family. A woman hired to help out took everyone's coats.

Giving Ivy a hug, Andy asked how she was doing with her parents.

"You were right. It's as if we've never been apart."

"I love that dress on you, Ivy."

"Thanks, Elena. You look like a model in that brocade jacket and jeans."

"One of my New York friends sent it to me to wear. She thought I'd look good in it."

"She was right." Ivy smiled, so glad Elena was keeping in touch with the girls from the city.

Everyone mingled. Ivy's parents remembered Murphy and his wife. They enjoyed catching up and hashing over stories about the village and some of its characters. Christmas Eve was off to a wonderful start. When a sleigh pulled by a reindeer stopped in front of a big bay window, excitement filled that farmhouse. Once that happy couple was inside enjoying some eggnog, the chef sent his staff around serving hors d'oeuvres. It felt like Times Square on New Year's Eve. Even better.

Ivy had instructed the chef to tell her when he was ready to serve dinner. When he did, it took a bit to get everyone seated. Once they were all settled, Ivy officially welcomed her guests to her home.

"Looking at all of your beautiful faces together on a Christmas Eve fills me with gratitude for the love shown me since I was a little girl. No matter where I've been in life, I've taken all of you with me. I consider us to be one big family, and now I invite you to relax and enjoy a fine meal with wonderful company. I wish you a very Merry Christmas."

With a wink to Doc and Vivian, Ivy sat down next to Andy to enjoy a dinner as fine and exquisite as any prepared in the city. A certain bowl caught her mother's eye.

"Oh, Ivy! Is that your gramma's Jewel bowl sitting there full of potatoes?"

"It is! That's my favorite bowl, Mom. I don't remember how I ended up with it, but I'm glad I did. This is such a special occasion that I wanted the bowl to be a part of our family getting back together. Think she bought it with her S&H Green Stamps?"

"If at all possible, she would have. She loved her green stamps," laughed Ivy's mother.

"What are green stamps?" Elena asked.

"Next time you're at the house, I'll show you my old Green Stamp books. I can't bring myself to throw them out," joked Vivian.

Conversation flowed as easy as the wine. One course after another was served. Time flew. Ivy knew she had to hurry them along. She went to the kitchen and spoke with the chef, who knew what was about to happen.

"It's getting late. I'll have everyone move into the front room by telling them that's where we'll be serving dessert. Little will they know; dessert is the fantastic wedding cake you created."

"You designed the cake, Ivy, right down to the edible chocolate reindeer topper."

"It had to be a reindeer, and Doc loves chocolate."

So that was the plan. When the tables were being cleared, Ivy made the announcement as Doc and Vivian disappeared.

"I don't know about any of you, but I need to stretch and move a little before dessert is served. How about we go in the front room? Whatever you might like to drink is already in there. Then we'll relax and enjoy dessert."

Everyone followed Ivy. No one caught on to how the chairs were arranged or how bouquets of Christmas flowers and poinsettias were placed about the room.

"I love that big window, Ivy. The sunsets must be breathtaking."

"That they are Murphy, especially now with the snow."

The string quartet took their place. No one questioned why. Instead, they enjoyed the music. Andy noticed his grandfather and Vivian were absent. He asked Ivy if she knew where they went.

"I think if you and Elena come over here with me, your question will be answered."

That was the clue for the string quartet to play the couple's entrance song. When Andy heard the beginning chords, he remarked it was Doc's favorite. Then he looked at Ivy, who had tears in her eyes. Then he looked at the doorway and realized what was about to happen as his grandfather and Vivian slowly made their way into the room, arm in arm, smiling, with Vivian holding a small bouquet of white Christmas orchids and wearing a deep purple dress she'd pulled out from her closet and beautifully reinvented with French lace. What started so very long ago at a soda fountain in a downtown full of memories was coming full circle at a farmhouse on Christmas Eve.

"Please stand, everyone," said Ivy, "as Doc and Vivian make their way into the room to say their wedding vows."

Joyous tears and looks of surprise were everywhere. As the justice of the peace took his place in front of the window, Doc and Vivian were joined by Andy and Elena. The four of them approached the justice. After heartache and making do, the couple said their vows written over the years.

"You may kiss the bride," instructed the justice of the peace.

Those tears of joy kept flowing as applause broke out. Louise covered her ears. Hazel jumped up and down as the newlyweds were embraced by those gathered, still in amazement of what had just taken place.

"I am so happy for you, Gramps. What a Christmas surprise!"

"Thank you, Elena. I am one lucky man."

"Yes, you are," replied Elena as she embraced Vivian.

"Grampa! Vivian! Congratulations. What a perfect time to get married. You both deserve great happiness."

"It was hard keeping it secret, Andy. I wanted to shout it out for all to hear that I was marrying the love of my life!"

Everyone cheered.

As guests mingled, champagne was served in crystal glasses by waiters wearing black dress pants, holiday-red long-sleeved shirts, and thin holly-green ties. Ivy had one of the waiters deliver a Santa mug half filled with punch to Hazel. The little girl was thrilled.

"Is this from Santa Claus?" she asked her aunt Ivy.

"Yes, it is, Hazel. When you are sound sleep, Santa will bring you presents."

"Mommy said he will leave us some in our fancy room. When we get home, we'll find more presents. Daddy said it will be like having two Christmases."

"Your daddy is right, and guess what, Hazel?" Ivy whispered.

"There are presents for you and Louise and Willie under that tree in the other room.

"I know how to spell my name, Aunt Ivy." With that statement, Hazel ran into that other room.

"Where is Hazel off to in such a hurry?"

"She's going to look for her name on gift tags on the presents under the tree."

"I remember doing that," said Andy. "I'd get so excited when I found my name."

Andy changed the subject. "Thank you for doing so much for Grampa and Vivian. You've made their wedding unforgettable."

"It's been my pleasure, Andy. They're both very special to me."

"I've been meaning to tell you something, Ivy. I just didn't know how to bring it up."

"You can tell me anything, Andy. You, too, are special to me."

"I feel awkward."

While Andy was the total opposite of John, Ivy had that same feeling she had when John was trying to get her to go back upstairs with him without giving any reason until she insisted. She felt she had to do the same thing now, no matter his answer.

"Tell me, Andy. I'm a big girl."

"I met a woman," he spitted out. "Well, actually, she brought her cat in and one thing led to another, and we've been seeing each other ever since."

While Ivy had no right to feel hurt, because they'd never actually dated or even gone beyond a kiss, she did feel weird. At first. But the more she thought about it, the more she realized there really was nothing to feel weird about because there was nothing going on between them and there never would be. The attraction was not there. If it were, Ivy knew she would have felt it. That's how she was wired. Just like Vivian.

This moment at hand was Ivy's off-ramp with Andy. And she took it.

"I am so happy for you, Andy."

"Really?"

"Of course. Why wouldn't I be?"

"Well, you and I, we're sort of …"

Andy got stuck. He was confused, like Ivy had been confused until she admitted to herself that there was no attraction between them.

"You said it, Andy. *We're sort of.* I've thought about you and me and I think what we share is a fondness for each other. It's not romantic, but at first, we thought it might be. If we are honest, it isn't, Andy. But I can say I love you because I do. I love you as a very dear and special friend. Please believe me, Andy, when I say I am so happy for you. I can't wait to meet her."

"Oh, Ivy, that's exactly how I feel about you and how I feel about us." Andy was so relieved that he took hold of Ivy and pulled her close. Seconds later, he whispered, "I took the liberty of asking her to stop by later, Ivy. I hope you don't mind. Oh, her name is Connie."

"I don't mind at all, Andy," Ivy replied. "Connie is more than welcome anytime."

With the champagne still flowing, Ivy told the chef it was time for dessert.

As soon as Hazel caught sight of a cake with a chocolate reindeer on top sitting in the middle of a fancy table on wheels, she jumped up and followed it into the front room. Ivy's mother saw her coming.

"Slow down, Hazel, or you'll be wearing that beautiful cake," she laughed, taking Hazel's hand.

"See the reindeer, Gramma?"

"I do. It's a chocolate reindeer."

"It's a magical reindeer. It's Christmas Eve."

Ivy's mother told Hazel how pretty she looked in her long candy cane dress with crinolines, making it look even prettier. When her mother picked Hazel up and went dancing and swirling in front of the big bay window showcasing twinkling stars and a silver moon on a most wondrous eve, Hazel laughed and giggled and hugged her grandmother.

Observing the two together reminded Ivy when she was the little girl being held by her mother as they danced and swirled about that double living room decked out with a Christmas tree that reached the ceiling.

166

"I love watching Mom with my children," said Izzie, now by Ivy's side. "Sometimes, like now, I feel as if I'm watching you and me. The feelings are the same. I treasure the memories of our Christmas Eves when Grandma and Grandpa would come for supper and the house smelled like her banana bread."

"Oh, yes, Izzie. Just like her banana bread! That's the only other thing I can cook!"

The sisters hugged as Hazel continued to be swirled about in her candy cane dress.

When the chef gave the okay, Ivy escorted the bride and groom over to their reindeer cake. Before cutting it, Doc had a few words to say.

"How do I begin to thank all of you gathered here to celebrate a wedding of two people young at heart and blessed with a love that has endured time and challenges, only to be rewarded by a chocolate reindeer? I dare say that was Ivy's idea."

Turning to Ivy, Doc thanked her for the time and effort she put into creating a Christmas Eve wedding they would never forget, adding, "Ivy was a clever little checkers player. But she's even better at creating wedding memories."

Holding up his glass of champagne with his bride by his side, Doc thanked Elena and Andy for always being there and Murphy and his family and Ivy's family for traveling to attend and lastly, he thanked Vivian.

"To my lovely bride, there are no words that can express my love for you."

Glasses were raised as the wedding cake was enjoyed. While Hazel would have loved that chocolate reindeer topper, Ivy took it back to the chef, who wrapped it up and put it in the refrigerator. It wasn't long before the dancing began.

When Connie arrived, she was welcomed with open arms. Then the dancing continued on. Ivy instantly liked the cute little blond. She thought Andy and Connie made a lovely couple.

"I've heard so much about you, Ivy. I can tell how much you mean to Andy," Connie said as they walked into what was now the party

167

room with its big window looking out over a field covered in snow under a spectacular moon.

"I feel the same about Andy. I am so happy you both met. Whenever I am here, you are more than welcome to stop in. But now we have some dancing to do."

"I heard that," laughed Murphy, taking Ivy's hand. "You owe me a dance from that night I found you sitting on a swing out in the snow."

"What a night that was, Murphy!"

"I know. Now let's go, Ivy!"

The two claimed the floor, jitterbugging, the faster the better. The string quartet amazed everyone with their abilities. When the tempo slowed down, a little girl giggling caught everyone's attention. Hazel kept it up. Despite her father telling her to quiet down, she couldn't. She had everyone laughing.

"What is so funny, Hazel?" Izzie asked. "What are you laughing at?"

Still laughing, she pointed to the window. "Look, Mommy. A reindeer is peeking in at me."

"A reindeer?"

"Yes! A big reindeer. He's peeking at me through the window. He is so funny."

Everyone looked. There was no sign of a reindeer outside until Doc stepped in front of the window.

That's when Walter appeared.

"Hazel is right," Doc declared.

"A mighty big reindeer is here."

Chapter Twenty-Four

Once Walter showed his face, the party was over.

Favorite cookies wrapped inside small brown paper bags were given out. Those who knew the tradition of the sour cream chocolate chip cookies couldn't believe Ivy had done the baking.

"When I first arrived, I caught the aroma of these cookies, but I told myself that was impossible," said Ivy's mom. "Then I found that glass plate full of them, but I didn't realize you did the baking. Thank you, Ivy. They were delicious. They bring back wonderful memories sitting on that vintage plate. It was so thoughtful of you to make them. I've missed you, Ivy."

"Your mother said it all, Ivy. They certainly do bring back memories of you and Izzie when you were little," said her father, smiling. "To repeat what your mother said, they are wonderful memories."

Everyone understood why Walter became the priority. Everyone knew how much Walter was loved. He was part of the family. Doc, with Andy's input, agreed Walter would be okay in Ivy's barn for a few nights. When Christmas was over, they'd move him back to Doc's. Consensus was, he still missed Pearl. He hadn't given that new rabbit a chance of becoming his friend.

Christmas morning found Walter still out of sorts. Ivy fed him and refreshed his water. She spent some time brushing him and talking to him before she met everyone at the hotel for breakfast. Hazel was in a hurry. She knew there were presents waiting for her at home.

"Mommy said after we open all of those presents, we can open the ones you gave us, Aunt Ivy. They are right beside me in the car."

"We'll call after we get home and they've opened their gifts," Izzie told Ivy as they were getting ready to leave.

Saying goodbye to everyone wasn't easy.

Ivy spent the rest of the day getting her home back in order. Then she did a little more work on the Elena Collection before getting ready to go to Vivian and Doc's for Christmas dinner. Upstairs, deciding what to wear, she happened to look out the window and noticed Doc's truck at the barn. She bundled up and went out to see him.

"Didn't I have breakfast with you earlier? For being a newlywed, you get around," joked Ivy.

"The only thing that could have pulled me away from my bride on Christmas is this old fella."

"It doesn't look like Walter has eaten very much or touched his water."

"I gave him a good checking just now. Maybe I'll wait a few more days and then check him again. We'll see. Do you mind if he stays a little longer?"

"Walter can move in as far as I'm concerned."

"He seems more comfortable here than in my new barn. Could be the smell of newness bothers him after living on the lane. Time will tell."

Noting the worry and sadness in Doc's tone, Ivy gave him a hug.

That's when Doc let his guard down.

Scratching his head, and then shrugging his shoulders, he looked at Ivy, and then turned away.

Staring down at the floor, clearing his throat, Doc opened up.

"I spoke with Noelene on my way here." Doc hesitated, moving in front of the window. Ivy stayed quiet.

The wind moving the snow up and around in little whirlwinds kept Doc's attention as he continued talking. "When Walter was younger and the only reindeer in my barn, we used to go for walks along the lane. Winter seemed to be his favorite time, especially when the wind would do what it's doing now with the snow. That Walter would kick up his hooves and push the snow and twirl about the lane. I used to tell him he was meant to be a dancing reindeer. Told him he'd be a big hit and I could make some good money off him. He seemed to understand. He'd twirl around even faster. How do I say goodbye to him, Ivy? He's part of my family."

Standing beside Doc, watching those little whirlwinds cross over the field, Ivy tried to comfort her friend.

"I remember the day my mother said I had to say goodbye to you because we'd be moving. She didn't say when. I learned it was a few days later. It was a Wednesday. I remember every detail, even what I was wearing and the weather and the feel of your tears falling on my hands when you spoke softly to me after our last game of checkers. I think you let me win every game we played that day, but winning at checkers couldn't take away the deep sadness I felt when walking down those front steps sobbing, feeling sick to my stomach, never looking back, flying into my house and up the stairs, into my room and then into my bed until the next day. My heart was broken. My head was aching. I remember lying on my bed during the night and staring over at your house as if I was taking photos to keep with me wherever life took me."

Snow buntings at the feeder interrupted the moment. Then Ivy continued.

"While that time was traumatic, what helped me through were the memories I had of you and me together. So many wonderful memories. Eventually those memories took away the sadness. You'll discover you have so many beautiful memories of time spent with Walter. That doesn't mean you won't shed some tears. I still do when I think back to you and me. But the tears are now happy tears, appreciative that I have those memories in my heart. They will be with me forever."

Without saying a word, Doc told hold of Ivy's hand. Watching the snow continue to swirl about, with tears falling on their hands, Doc told Ivy what he really planned on doing.

"I'm taking Walter back home. He's telling me it is time."

Doc broke down. Ivy was there to catch him and hold him and listen.

"Noelene has a place for him by the same window he'd look out years ago. It's the same barn with the same smells and feels and sounds he'll remember. It'd be like you moving back to your house on the lane. Despite updates and changes made over the years, those sounds and smells remain as they were. They're in the fabric of that home just like they are in Walter's first home. He can look out the same window and see things with his tired eyes that he saw in his youth. He'll be able to rest and be in peace."

"Taking Walter back home is the best thing you can do for him. There's no pill that can bring real peace of mind like that of being at peace because of your surroundings and love of others. When are you leaving for Noelene's?"

"She's making train reservations on her Reindeer Flyer Express for the twenty-eighth. I just have to get him to the station and staff will be there to help get him on the train and make him comfortable for the trip. There will be a place for me to stay near him all the way up north. I return on the twenty-ninth. I called Andy after confirming with Noelene. He agrees it is the best for Walter. He is going to tell Elena."

"Did Andy say anything about accompanying you on the journey?"

"Yes. He wanted to go, but I told him he and Elena would be better off saying goodbye to Walter now. I don't want to have to deal with them when I myself have to say goodbye to my dear friend. That will be hard enough. It might sound selfish, but it's how it has to be. Vivian offered to go but admitted it would be hard the way her legs tire easily. It's for the best. Knowing she is at home waiting for me is all I need."

Now the chickadees were at the feeder.

"Look at that. The chickadees and snow buntings are having a snack together. Life is in the small things, Ivy."

Glancing over at Doc, his face lined with wrinkles and his eyes red from crying and his wild white hair all over the place and still within him a heart full of life and loving, Ivy quietly offered to accompany him to Noelene's.

"I won't get in your way or tell you what to do. I won't cause a scene. I won't pester you when you want to be alone. I'll simply be there like you've always been there for me."

The sun broke though the whirlwinds. Doc held Ivy's hand even tighter.

"The train leaves at seven thirty. I'll tell Noelene you will be accompanying me."

Chapter Twenty-Five

Dinner that night at Doc and Vivian's was a quiet one after a discussion about Walter leaving on the twenty-eighth was underway. Ivy tried changing the subject with remarks about the newlywed's home or property or even Vivian's obvious touches. But the thought of Walter going on a train and never coming back was too much to shove aside. The conversation eventually led to telling Walter stories. Of course, Doc had many to tell. So did Andy and Elena. Vivian had one to tell, one precious story about that mighty reindeer. After clearing the table covered in one of her finest linens, apple pie with vanilla ice cream along with fresh-perked coffee was served. As they enjoyed their dessert, Vivian told her story as if she and Doc were the only ones in the room.

"When you called one Sunday to say you were under the weather and wouldn't be picking me up to go to our weekly spaghetti dinner at the diner, I thought I'd bring you some of my homemade vegetable soup. I'd made it the night before because I felt a sore throat coming. The soup was my supper. When I woke up that Sunday morning, I felt wonderful. No hint of a sore throat, so I was hoping the soup would help you feel better. While my shop was closed, I was there doing paperwork. I left early. Stopped at my place to get you the soup. Then

I continued to your home. When you didn't answer the front door, I went to the door facing the lane and still no answer. I saw a light on in your barn, so I walked down the lane, still carrying the pot of soup. The door wasn't secured so I knocked a few times, but no answer. As I turned to leave, I thought I saw someone move toward the back, so I knocked again. And Walter appeared. While I'd never met him before, you'd told me so many stories about him that I was certain the reindeer standing in front of me was the infamous Walter. What gave him away were the reindeer decorations hanging from his antlers. You'd tell me stories about them too. He came to the door, and I knew in his own way he was inviting me in. So, I accepted his invitation."

Vivian's story was changing everyone's mood from gloom to laughter.

"I can see that Walter taking charge all decked out in his finest attire," Doc roared.

"What happened once you were inside the barn?" Elena asked.

"Walter stepped back so I could get in and shut the door. Then he noticed I was carrying something. He came over and smelled it. Then he licked my hands. I considered that to be his seal of approval. We both stood looking at each other until I had the craziest thought. I wondered if I asked where you were, he might let me know."

"Good thinking, Vivian. If that had been me, his sheer size would have intimidated me. I probably never would have opened the door."

"That did go through my mind, Ivy, but when I looked into his eyes, I saw a gentle soul. I also remembered those stories Doc told me about him, and not a one depicted Walter as anything but a kind and, at times, funny reindeer."

"There's no finer reindeer than Walter."

"I would add to that, Doc. There's no finer or hungrier reindeer than Walter," Vivian added.

"Well, he does like to eat."

"I found that out, honey. Now back to my story. I decided to ask him where you were, and that son of a gun turned around and started walking further into the barn. When I just stood there, he stopped, turned back around and looked at me as if to say, 'Come on.' So, I put the soup down on a table and off I went, following Walter. To my surprise, he led me right to you. I couldn't see you at first because you were wrapped up in layers of blankets. I knew you were there because you were snoring. I thanked Walter. Then I turned my attention to you. I couldn't fully wake you up. I figured you must have had the chills because of all the blankets on you. I checked for a fever. Nothing. After sitting there for a few minutes, I decided it would be best to write you a note and leave it by the pot of soup. Problem with that was, by the time I got back toward the front of the barn, the pot was empty. Not one drop was left, and that mighty reindeer decked out in reindeer decorations was sound asleep. I never wrote the note. I picked up my empty pot, opened the door, shut it, walked up the lane, got in my car, and went home to bed, wishing I had some of that homemade vegetable soup to enjoy."

"You never said a thing to me about Walter and the soup."

"I didn't want to get him in trouble, Doc."

"Well, that was some story," laughed Andy. "Walter has brought us so many good times."

"First, I lost Pearl. Now Walter is leaving. I would really like to go with you, Gramps."

"I ask for your understanding, Elena. Walter's leaving is hard on all of us."

Hugging her Gramps, Elena told him she understood.

"You are learning the irony of life, young lady. One minute life can bring great joy. Then out of the blue, life can bring you to your knees in sadness or despair. But always remember, life is a beautiful gift. After all, life brought us Walter."

As Doc enjoyed another slice of apple pie, the question of how to get Walter to the train station was discussed.

"We were able to get all our reindeer out of one barn and into another. Certainly, we can get Walter on a train," Andy said. "I'll go with you to Ivy's tomorrow afternoon, Doc, to pick Walter up. Then I'll help you get him to the train station early the next morning."

"I will say my goodbyes in the barn, Dad. Just me and Walter."

"I think that's best, Elena."

After thanking Doc and Vivian for a lovely evening, Ivy said good night to Andy and Elena.

"Thank you for being so welcoming to Connie last night, Ivy."

"She is lovely, Andy. I am happy for you."

Embracing Elena, Ivy told her it might be helpful if she made Walter a new reindeer decoration. "I'm certain he can tell when he's wearing one, and I'm sure he knows who put it there."

"It was silly of me to make those. He's a reindeer, not a person."

"Walter is a very perceptive reindeer. Doc showed me a few photos of him wearing some reindeer decorations. In every one he holds his head high as he appears to be prancing along. Those decorations would be like us wearing earrings. They give him a little bling. As far as you making a new decoration, I find using my hands to create something calms me down. It helps to put things in perspective. When I get back home tonight, I'll work on the Elena Collection. There's no better way to make sense of the world than by creating something beautiful."

Ivy not only worked on the Elena Collection when she got back home, she was working on it again early the following morning after spending time with Walter. The knot in her stomach was getting tighter. Thanks to a phone call midmorning, her focus changed for a moment.

"Lawrence. So glad you called."

Ivy took a minute to update Lawrence on Walter and the wedding. Then she got down to business. "I'm working on our Elena Collection. I love it already."

"That's wonderful, Ivy. I wish you the best with Walter. He sounds like a very special reindeer."

"As Doc would say, they all are, Lawrence."

"Doc would know more than most people. I enjoyed spending what time I could with him when he came to New York. Please tell him I'm thinking about all of you."

"I sure will, Lawrence. Thanks."

"I won't keep you, Ivy. You must have enough to do before catching that train. I wanted to update you on the Cannes event coming up in June. I'd appreciate seeing any sketches you can send me. I had a call about new bolts of fabric coming in, so I thought I'd take a look. This time of year remains about the busiest."

Ivy could tell Lawrence was in one of his moods to talk. Ivy wasn't. She cut the call short before he took off on a tangent. Then she hurried upstairs to take a shower. She planned on packing a bag for her trip up north later on. Warmth would be the criteria for anything she chose to take. Around three o'clock, she heard Doc's truck pulling up to the barn. Walter's life was about to take a drastic turn. Ivy hurried out the back door.

When Ivy walked into the barn, she could tell Doc was in a sour mood. It took him a few minutes to open up.

"Elena wants to say her goodbye to Walter tonight. I told her not to upset him by crying. I could tell she took offense at what I had to say, but Walter saw enough crying when we lost Pearl."

"I talked to Elena again this morning, Grampa. She understands and intends to give Walter a hug and then leave," Andy explained, leading Walter toward the door.

"I don't like coming down so hard on Elena, Andy. I know how much she loves the animals, but my focus must be on what is best for Walter," Doc added, following behind the reindeer.

Ivy was thankful Walter didn't give them a problem getting in the hauler. Both Doc and Andy were having a tough time. While Andy tended to Walter, Doc spent the time with Ivy.

"Remember my kitten, Doc? When we lived next door, someone ran her over? You saw it happen, picked her up, and hurried to your barn, but by the time you got there, my kitten had died."

"She was a puffball, Ivy. Orange with streaks of white. When she passed, that little kitten looked as if she was sound asleep."

"You remember her, Doc?"

"I remember all the animals brought to me. You see, our family is a rather large family."

With Walter secure, plans were made for morning. Ivy would be meeting them at the train station by six fifteen.

Back in the kitchen, Ivy grabbed something to eat with a cup of tea and took it with her upstairs to pack her bag. That didn't take long. After working on more sketches and messaging Lawrence, Ivy went to bed.

Chapter Twenty-Six

WALTER WAS ON THE TRAIN WHEN Ivy arrived at the station. He had his own window to look out, with fresh hay and water nearby. Ivy was happy to see a knitted decoration hanging from where one of his antlers had been before losing them.

"What time did you and Doc get here?" she asked Andy.

"Doc called me at three thirty. He couldn't sleep. I asked him if he wanted to get going, and about half an hour later, I was at his place. Walter gave us no problems. The train had arrived by the time we got here, so we were able to get him on board without rushing him."

Looking at Walter through the window, Ivy could tell he was scared. She could see it in his eyes.

"He looks exhausted."

"He is, just like Doc."

"I'll keep my eye on Doc, so don't worry about him. It's a good thing we return tomorrow."

"I think so too. Getting Walter back up north has been on his mind."

"I love Elena's decoration."

"I'm not sure what Noelene will think about it."

"Something tells me she will love it after she hears the story behind it."

Tickets were not needed. Passengers were on a list approved by Noelene. Once Ivy was checked off that list, she followed Andy up a few stairs and into the train. It wasn't your regular passenger train. It was strictly for the movement of Noelene's reindeer. Each reindeer had its own space aboard the Reindeer Flyer Express. If accompanied by anyone specific, an area in front of where the reindeer was situated was reserved for that person or persons. Noelene made sure that space was complete with pillows, blankets, a large sofa, comfortable chairs, reading material, and a coffee nook.

No devices were allowed. None.

A short gentleman resembling a conductor out of a movie back in the forties, with a hat that looked too big for him and a double-breasted coat with wool pants rolled up on the bottom, blew his whistle.

"I hereby announce the Reindeer Flyer Express will be leaving the station in twenty minutes. Please check your reindeer for all safety requirements as posted in each reindeer area. Conditions are good. We should arrive on time. Feel free to make your own coffee. Pastries and sandwiches are in the refrigerator in the area assigned you. For those staying the night, the Reindeer Inn is down the street from the train station. A coffee/malt shop is next door. Over the years other shops have opened. All are friendly and understanding of the story of the reindeer. A library is the focal point of our community. Enjoy your time on the Flyer Express. For those not traveling with us today, please say your goodbyes now and exit the train. To those interested in other trains coming and going, please check inside the station."

"I think that's my signal to leave. Love you, Grampa. You are doing what's best for Walter. I'll be thinking of you two." Hesitating, Andy quickly added, "Thanks, Ivy."

He didn't stick around for any replies. He didn't look at Walter as he exited the train.

The short gentleman with the oversized hat blew his whistle again. The train slowly started to move. Walter kept looking out the window.

"Hear ye! Hear ye! Welcome aboard the Reindeer Flyer Express. My name is Whitaker. I will be coming around to welcome the reindeer individually."

Pulling out a green velvet pouch from a pocket in his double-breasted coat, Whitaker began to go from one train car to the next. Ivy felt her heart go a little faster. *Surely that pouch made of green velvet can't be mine? No! Never! It can't be mine!*

From what Ivy could tell, there were seven reindeer in all. Walter's car was third in line. As the anticipation built, Walter stood with his head held high.

"That's the first time that darn reindeer has done that in a long while, standing there as proud as the young buck that he was when he came to live in my barn on the lane. What with the smells of the train and the wood and the oils and grease and the steam and the creaking and the wheels grinding along the tracks, I'm thinking he is remembering. He is going back to another barn far, far away."

It wasn't long before the door opened. It was Walter's turn to be welcomed back home. Whitaker spoke directly to Doc.

"I can tell you have taken care of this mighty reindeer in the manner expected. As you are aware, reindeer possess a bit of magic. The Legend of the Reindeer, passed down through generations professes reindeer magic is stirred by the snow, considered to be quite mystical, and the wind considered to be quite enchanting, and the gift of a child's imagination considered to be the purest of the pure. Such magic is a gift to be shared as only a reindeer can on the eve of Christmas."

Smiling, Whitaker continued as he turned and spoke to Walter.

"You have shared your gift with the children. Now it is time to rest in the beauty of the mountains from which you came."

Remaining tall and proud, Walter stood still as Whitaker opened his green velvet pouch and pulled out a handful of bits of pinecones and pine needles as well as needles from hemlock trees and scotch pines. With a thrust of his hand, Whitaker released the needles and pinecones as far above Walter as he could. Then he bowed his head in silence as the train kept moving up the mountain.

"Welcome home, Walter."

After greeting the mighty reindeer, Whitaker pulled tight the ties of the green velvet pouch, and as he did, Ivy wondered. She had to find out.

"May I ask a question, Whitaker?"

"Yes, certainly, Ivy."

"I was admiring the green velvet evening bag you carry the pine needles and such in. Where did it come from, or do you know who made it? I'd love to buy one to take back with me."

"There is a story attached to what we call the green velvet pouch. Noelene used to go to a pine grove to pick needles to make pillows. One day she couldn't find the old pouch she'd normally take with her. She happened to mention it to the new owner of our local coffee shop. She asked if maybe someone found it and turned it in. This must have been ten or so years ago. Well, that young man jumped up, went in the back room, and returned with this velvet pouch. He handed it to Noelene and told her to keep it. When Noelene asked where he got it, because she, like you, Ivy, said she'd like to buy some to have on hand, he told her it had been found in a snowbank."

"Where? Did he say where?"

"Not that I ever heard. But you can ask him. He still works at the coffee shop. His name is Danny. He's there most every day."

Once Walter was settled for the night, Ivy and Doc headed to the inn. On the way, Doc suggested she ask Vivian to make her a green velvet evening bag like the one Whitaker was holding.

"Vivian already made me one."

"Well then, why do you need another?"

"Because I lost it, Doc, and that guy named Danny found it."

"What?"

"That evening bag Whitaker had is mine."

"How can you tell?"

"Vivian surprised me with the green velvet evening bag to go with my gown. To give it a little class, she embroidered small, cranberry hearts near the bottom so they'd show when I pulled the strings tight. That evening bag Whitaker had is mine. It has those small cranberry hearts around the bottom. I know that's it, Doc. I remember that shade of cranberry, thinking I'd like to find some velvet that shade for another dress."

"What can we do, Ivy?"

"Right now, we have to check into our rooms and get some sleep. While you visit with Noelene tomorrow, I'm going to introduce myself to this Danny person and get the story about my green velvet evening bag."

The inn was quite charming. Ivy loved her room, complete with a queen-size bed with a feather mattress and a view of the mountains like something out of a movie. Adding to the moment was the snow falling and the moon peeking between the clouds. With no devices to play on and no TV to get lost in, Ivy fell sound asleep on her feather mattress wondering about that green velvet evening bag and the guy who found it.

Chapter Twenty-Seven

Doc and Ivy met in the dining room for breakfast. While a fire in the fireplace crackled and a light snow fell, coffee was served in stoneware mugs. A matching stoneware serving plate held a variety of delicious French croissants, some almond filled, some jam filled, and some chocolate filled. Some were plain. When omelets were served with a side of French toast sprinkled with confectionery sugar, Doc had to laugh.

"Vivi would be surprised at the amount I am eating. It must be the mountain air."

"I'm on my second croissant and still have an omelet to go," laughed Ivy. "Lawrence would be shocked."

"With our train leaving at three, this meal will hold me until I get back home to my bride."

"What time do you meet with Noelene?"

"It was supposed to be at eleven, but I had a call just before I left the room saying Noelene would prefer to meet with me at one, so that's what I'll do. She extended the invitation to you as well."

"Wonderful. I would love to meet her."

"When I leave here, I'm going to stay with Walter until I see Noelene. Hard to believe our remaining time together is down to hours."

"You've given him your time since you first met. Walter knows how much you love him."

"I just remembered something, Ivy. I left Elena's decoration hanging where one of Walter's antlers sat."

"There is a lovely story behind that decoration."

"True. I bet it will be the first reindeer decoration Noelene has ever seen."

After a third cup of coffee, they went their separate ways. Ivy told Doc she was going to walk around and end up at the coffee shop before returning for their meeting with Noelene.

It had stopped snowing. The sun shining above the mountains made the landscape sparkle as Ivy took her time going down the snowy cobblestone sidewalk. After doing some window shopping, Ivy crossed the street. Taking a deep breath, she approached the coffee shop. Whatever their brand of coffee, Ivy was hooked on it the moment she walked inside. The aroma was heavenly.

The place was crowded. Ivy had to wait in line for a coffee. When it was her turn to order, she asked for a small latte, then added, "Is Danny in?"

"Yes. He's out back with a salesman."

"Mind if I wait?"

"Not at all. If you give me your name, I'll let him know you are here."

"We've never met. I just have a question."

"Please wait a minute."

The young man hurried through a doorway. Then he hurried right back. "Danny will be with you in a moment. You can't miss him."

The young man didn't give any details, so Ivy stepped aside and waited.

When a big burley guy with Elvis sideburns appeared in the doorway, searching the crowd, Ivy walked over.

"Danny?"

"Yes. Are you the young woman looking for me?"

"I am. Do you have a moment?"

"I do. What can I help you with, miss?"

"My name is Ivy. I am about to catch the train. Before I leave, I must ask you something."

"You've stirred my curiosity, Ivy."

"I'll only take a moment. I can see how busy you are." With Danny standing there staring at her, Ivy blurted it out. "Where did you get the green velvet evening bag?"

"What?"

"The green velvet evening bag Whitaker uses on the Reindeer Flyer Express. Where did you find it?"

"I don't know what you are talking about."

"Whitaker keeps bits of pine needles and twigs in it. You know, on the train with the reindeer."

"You mean Noelene's Whitaker?"

"Yes."

"Okay, now I understand. I remember seeing the sadness in Noelene's eyes one particular morning when she came in for a coffee and told me about losing the pouch used to collect the twigs and needles to bless her old reindeer. I hurried into the kitchen and came back with the green velvet pouch. I was going to give it to my niece, but I decided it belonged with Noelene. It was the least I could do considering the care she gives those reindeer."

"Where did you find it?"

"I didn't."

"Who gave it to you?"

"A fella I know."

"Who?"

"That guy sitting right over there by the door at that round table. His name is Nicholas. He owns the place. He bought it from me."

"Thank you, Danny. By the way, you serve delicious coffee."

Pointing out the window, Danny replied, "There's magic in those mountains. Nice meeting you, Ivy."

Working her way through the crowd, Ivy tried to get a look at Nicholas, but his back was to her. She slowly made her way around the table. He was reading a newspaper.

"Excuse me, Nicholas?"

He didn't hear her. The place was noisy. She suddenly wanted to leave until the stranger put the newspaper down. When he looked into her eyes, all Ivy could think about was the moment Vivian met Doc in the malt shop.

"That particular day the place was crowded," Vivian had told Ivy. "All the tables were taken. I decided to leave and come back later, but a handsome man with a pleasant smile asked if I'd like to sit with him. Oh, Ivy. I was so hesitant. I swore I'd never have anything to do with a man again, but there was something about him. When he complimented me on my dress, I about cried."

At that very moment in a coffee shop in the mountains, Ivy got it. She understood what Vivian was saying. Despite telling John off in her studio at that charity event and telling Andy she took care of another loose end, way down deep inside, she hadn't. While she may have sounded certain that night, way down deep, she wasn't. Being so cruelly treated like a piece of meat in front of her peers and strangers, Ivy swore never again would she make herself vulnerable to anyone, but now, when this stranger looked into her eyes, smiled, introduced himself, and then complimented Ivy on her long, camel coat, all of that crap finally melted away. She about cried, just like Vivian about cried so many years before.

"I'm Ivy Nolan. Nice to meet you, Nicholas."

"You are welcome to join me, Ivy. It's pretty busy here this morning. Not many places to sit down and enjoy a cup of coffee."

Ivy was certain she heard a philharmonic playing somewhere. There had to be. No one had ever pronounced her name so beautifully.

Once she was seated, he continued. "Are you from the area? I know I would have remembered seeing you in here."

"No," Ivy replied, trying to get her head on. "I'm not from here. I came with an old friend on Noelene's train."

"That Noelene is one special lady. I've written about her before."

"You are a writer?"

"I freelance when I'm not buying coffee beans or sitting here reading my own story."

"I have a story to tell, Nicholas, and you might be a part of it. I believe you found something that belonged to me years ago." Ivy couldn't believe she was so blunt. But time was limited.

"Okay, Ivy. You have my attention. Tell me your story."

Ivy tried to keep it short. When she paused, Nicholas asked if she'd like another cup of coffee.

"I'd love one."

"I'll be right back," he replied, brushing against her when getting up.

Minutes later, Ivy was bringing Whitaker into the story.

"When I saw him pull out a green velvet evening bag full of twigs and needles from his pocket, I became curious. When I noted the embroidered hearts near the bottom, I was convinced that was my evening bag. Somehow in all the confusion that night in the hotel, I lost that bag. Does any of what I've said ring a bell with you?"

"I found that green velvet, as you say, evening bag in a snow pile down the street from the hotel. For some reason I picked it up and took a good look at it under the streetlight. My reporter's instinct at age twenty-one was developing. I'd just been hired by a small newspaper. I became inquisitive. From the intricate stitching around the bottom, I knew the bag wasn't from a discount store, so I decided to keep it."

"That's my hometown. I don't recall ever seeing you around."

"I was with my family. That's my mom's hometown. We were there visiting relatives before Christmas. The next day I went around that area asking if anyone owned the evening bag. I even went to the hotel and asked for the manager, but he was off that day. I was told he'd had a late night. I didn't have time to go back again before we left so I stuffed the bag in my backpack and it stayed there throughout the years. A few times I thought about tossing it, but that velvet bag grew to mean something to me. I had no clue what. When Danny and I were finalizing the sale of this place I reached inside my backpack, which was on its last leg by then, and happened to pull out the velvet pouch. Danny loved it. He offered to buy it for his niece, but I gave it to him. I had the feeling that's what I was supposed to do. It was time to let it go. So that's what I did."

"What an amazing story, Nicholas. That evening bag had quite the journey. I agree it is right where it belongs."

"Tell me a little about yourself."

Ivy didn't get to say too much. Doc walked in.

"Sorry to interrupt, Ivy. Noelene wants to see us right away."

Jumping up from the table, Ivy extended her had to Nicholas. "Thanks for letting me interrupt you, Nicholas. And thanks for telling me that unbelievable story. I'm thinking I dropped the evening bag in the snow when walking into the hotel."

"I have another theory, Ivy Nolan. I think that evening bag had one purpose and one purpose only."

"What do you mean?" Ivy asked, pushing her chair in.

Standing, holding her hand, Nicholas explained. "I believe that evening bag was meant to bring us together."

Doc was in a rush to get back.

"I have to go, Nicholas."

"Ivy! Noelene is waiting."

"Coming, Doc."

"Wait!"

Ivy was certain Nicholas's smile could have melted the snow outside.

"Before you leave me, tell me your favorite song, Ivy."

"What?""

"Your favorite song. What is your favorite song?"

"Ivy!"

"Coming, Doc."

Turning, Ivy embraced this stranger. "Silent Night!"

"I knew, I just knew you'd love a Christmas classic, Ivy Nolan, just like I do."

Out the door she flew. Nicholas followed. "Ivy!"

She kept going.

He kept yelling. "Ivy! That guy was crazy for leaving you!"

She never looked back. Tears were falling like snowflakes.

Chapter Twenty-Eight

MINUTES LATER, IVY WAS PULLING HERSELF together. Taking deep breaths.

"Sorry, Doc."

"Want to talk about it?"

"Not yet. Really. I'm okay."

As Ivy and Doc were walking up the front steps of the Reindeer Clinic, they noticed a few reindeer being led around a paddock. Each had its own handler. Off in a distant field, sleighs pulled by reindeer were sauntering along.

"Noelene mentioned the reindeer get daily exercise if they are up to it."

"What a special place, Doc. It must give you peace of mind knowing the attention Walter will receive. How was he when you visited him earlier?"

"He seemed to be rested from his journey. I could tell by the look on his face that he was content. That might have been because of the rabbits he was watching running around outside."

"Oh, I'm so glad he saw the rabbits, Doc."

"He was amused. It was fun watching him. So, Ivy, getting back to Walter being content, you and that young man sitting together in the coffee shop looked pretty content. Both of you seemed to be into the conversation. Had you ever met him before? I don't mean to prod. It's because I consider you more of a daughter than a friend. I want to protect you, Ivy."

"It's a long story, Doc. He's the one who found my green velvet evening bag."

"It sounds like another wild chapter in the long life of that dress you and Vivi made. What matters is that the evening bag was found."

"I can't wait to tell her. The guy's name is Nicholas. He found it in a snowbank."

"Get ready. You know Vivi will have lots of questions."

Once inside, they were escorted to a room with a fireplace and comfortable chairs and a window showcasing the splendor of the mountains. A few minutes later, the door opened and Noelene walked in with a young woman at her side.

"Welcome back, Doc. It's so nice to see you. This is my assistant, Lydia. And this must be Ivy," said Noelene, extending her hand. "It's very nice to meet you."

"It's a pleasure meeting you. May I call you Noelene?"

"Yes, of course."

The two sat down.

"I've spent some time with Walter. I can tell he's had a fine life with you, Doc. The sadness in your eyes reveals how much you've loved him over the years. Your tears tell me Walter will forever be in your heart. I only have one question. Why is there a decoration hanging on one of his antler stubs?"

Clearing his throat, shifting about his chair, Doc attempted to explain.

"Elena, my creative granddaughter, adores Walter. She'd spend a lot of time with him. Sometimes taking him for walks and sometimes brushing him. She recently helped Walter get over the death of his friend, Pearl, a fluffy white rabbit with a pink nose who was hit by a vehicle while crossing over to the other side of the lane. Walter was the first one there and the last one to leave.

One Christmas Elena decided Walter needed some Christmas cheer, so she knitted him his very own reindeer decorations. Oh, Noelene, you should have seen the two of them together out in the barn when they decided it was time to decorate where his antlers had been. Walter would sit very still and very proud as Elena decked him out in his Christmas decorations. Then they'd go strutting down the lane. That Walter would lift his hoofs as if he was prancing to music. Anyone they passed by loved Walter the dressed-up reindeer.

Doc started laughing. Then the laughing turned to tears.

"I didn't mean to do this. When the train was coming to a stop, I told myself I would not cry in front of anyone, especially Walter. But it's hard. That old reindeer is family. He cared about the other animals. He cared about all of us. The way he smiled when I'd scratch his back was his way of saying thank you. When it was just the two of us, at night, out in the barn, I'd be talking to him even when he was sleeping. Walter is great company. But this change in Walter's life is not about me, it is about him, and I am grateful my old friend is back in his mountains. Even a reindeer deserves to go back home when it is time."

Quietness came over that room as the sun disappeared in a sudden snow squall. Getting up from her chair, Noelene walked over to the window.

"I can still remember the first time I saw snow falling. My mother would always say I was five, but I still say I was four. It was close to midnight. For some reason I woke up from a sound sleep and looked out the window. Snowflakes were swirling by. I jumped up and ran over to get a closer look. It was snowing hard. The streetlights made the snowflakes glisten. I was so excited that I ran down the front stairs. I knew how to unlock the door, so out I went, barefoot and in my pajamas. As I stood on the front porch, mesmerized by the snow, a man and a woman went by in a cutter pulled by a reindeer. That was the moment I fell in love with reindeer. I went running down the street after the cutter until I felt my father's arms around me. He wrapped me up in his parka. He wasn't mad."

"I too love the snow," my father told me as he carried me into the house. "It's as magical as the reindeer that just passed you by."

"I believe there are turning points in our lives," Noelene continued. "My father put into words what I was feeling at such a young age. That feeling shaped my life. It's with me every day. But that is enough of my rambling on. Let us discuss those reindeer decorations."

The wise old woman with her long, gray hair pulled back in a braid, a shawl wrapped around her shoulders, and silver earrings dangling, sat back down and started laughing.

"For the life of me, Doc, I have never seen reindeer decked out for Christmas with knitted ornaments hanging from where their antlers had been."

"The decorations are very lightweight. I never would have allowed Elena to hang anything that was heavy on Walter's antlers."

Looking Doc straight in the eye, Noelene replied, "From the moment we first spoke, I sensed your goodness. I salute your Elena. For that young lady to even bother with Walter tells me she has inherited your gift of loving the reindeer. To tell me they grieved together over your Pearl confirms a decision I made this morning after seeing Walter dressed up in his decoration."

Noelene leaned over and whispered in Lydia's ear. Seconds later, the young woman stood and walked out of the room.

"Lydia will be right back. By the way, Doc, Lydia is my granddaughter."

As the sun returned, the door opened. In walked Lydia with a precious little reindeer following behind. Stopping in front of Noelene, Lydia picked the reindeer up and put her in Noelene's lap.

No one made a sound except for the wind.

"I'd like you to meet Douglas, named after the clump of Douglas firs out in the woods where he was found alone not long ago. We are not sure what happened to his mother. I can only assume he has lost her. In caring for Douglas, I've noticed great similarities between him and Walter when Walter was his age. As I once told you, Doc, we strive to find our little ones places where they can grow surrounded by love. I have never known a reindeer receiving such love and attention as Walter did with you. Hearing about your Elena and her reindeer decorations solidifies my decision way back when to place Walter with you. Now, I would like to give you Douglas. You may take him home today, and when he is ready to come back, the reindeer train will pick him up. An important note I must add." Noelene spoke directly to Doc, "Douglas is not a replacement for Walter. I'd be placing Douglas with you because of how Walter was adored by you and your family. Having your son, Andy, a veterinarian, is an added reason. One more thing. I can imagine Douglas adorned in Elena's reindeer decorations. Such a lucky little reindeer Douglas would be, going from loss to love. Such a precious gift you offer, Doc. Such a precious gift."

Doc's reply was spontaneous. "Your trust is my reason for accepting your gift, Noelene. Douglas will receive the love and care, and most likely the reindeer decorations, in the same manner as Walter did. I do not look at Douglas as a replacement for Walter, simply because Walter can never be replaced."

Getting up from his chair, Doc went over to meet Douglas. The little reindeer licked Doc's hands and nuzzled up against his jacket. Watching Doc interact with Douglas reminded Ivy of the times Doc would sit in his chair on the front porch of his house and smile as she contemplated her next move on the checkers board. She knew it wasn't the move that made him smile. It was their being together that mattered.

"I think this is another match made in heaven," said Noelene.

Doc did not reply. He was too busy getting to know Douglas.

Chapter Twenty-Nine

LYDIA WAS CALLED OUT OF THE room by a tall man dressed like a tin soldier. She returned a few minutes later and whispered something to Noelene.

"Thank you, Lydia."

Noelene stood in front of her two guests and made an announcement.

"Lydia relayed a message to me from the conductor of the Reindeer Flyer Express. He feels the train must leave early. By early, I mean momentarily. The snow is predicted to turn into a blizzard, and when we get a blizzard, everything stops, even the trains."

"No problem. We can go back to the inn, grab our bags, and be at the station in minutes."

"No need for you to go to the inn, Doc. I will have your bags picked up. I feel it is important that you are the one carrying Douglas into the station and onto the train. It will help build the trust he puts in you. I would suggest holding him as much as possible on your journey back home. I will take Douglas for a moment. There are a few staff members who would like to say goodbye to him. I will meet you both in the lobby. I have some things to pack for the little reindeer."

Knowing how fast snow can turn into a blizzard, Noelene was back within minutes as a van pulled up out front. Lydia followed with Douglas

Handing a bag of items to Ivy, Noelene mentioned a few items she'd included. "You'll find some beet pulp and concentrated feed. Both are good in a reindeer's winter diet. I'm sure you have access to both, Doc. Also included is Douglas's favorite blanket and, believe it or not, a rubber ball. He doesn't chew it. He looks for it at nighttime. I haven't figured out why, but I thought he'd need it a little longer. And here is an evening bag full of a variety of pine needles, Ivy. The smells will comfort him when falling asleep."

Ivy couldn't believe it. Noelene had given her the green velvet evening bag with cranberry hearts around the bottom. That bag had come full circle. When looking at Noelene for an explanation, the wise old woman merely winked.

Giving Doc a hug, she took Douglas from the arms of her assistant and placed the little reindeer in Doc's. "Go with Doc, my blessed Douglas. May your life be full. Your mother would have wanted nothing less for you."

Squeezing Doc's hands and hugging Ivy, Noelene turned and started walking down the hallway. She didn't get far before turning back around.

"Do not worry about your dear Walter, Doc. I've been told he had a good sleep. That is a wonderful start. And Ivy, you can thank Nicholas for that beautiful velvet evening bag. He just told me it belonged to you. My love to all."

Noelene continued down the hallway as the tin solider escorted Ivy and Doc out to the van. Douglas never flinched as they started off on yet another journey.

When passing by the coffee shop, Ivy was certain she spotted Nicholas walking up the cobblestone sidewalk. It was hard to tell since it was snowing. As the van moved passed the man, Ivy tried to get a closer look, but the van sped up and out of sight.

Thanks to Noelene, they escaped the blizzard. Douglas slept most of the way. As they got closer to home, Doc and Ivy discussed their quick trip and the reindeer asleep in Doc's arms.

"I can't wait to see everyone's reactions to Douglas. They will be so surprised."

"No more than I am, Ivy. A small part of me almost refused him. I think it was a loyalty thing I had going on in my head concerning Walter. But once Noelene put this little one in my arms, I realized bringing him home with me is what Walter would have wanted me to do. Caring for God's creatures is a part of living. Oh, I can see Elena now. She'll be getting her knitting needles out tonight."

They were getting closer.

Doc continued. "I'm thankful Andy is now the veterinarian. I am no spring chicken. I will encourage him to spend time with Douglas."

"You're not going anywhere, Doc."

"I learned when I lost my boy none of us know when our time will come. Age does not matter. That's why it's important that we live life instead of watching it pass us by. And that brings me back to that young man in the coffee shop. Tell me more about him."

"I'd just met him. The place was crowded, so he invited me to sit down for a cup of coffee. He owns the place. He's the one who found the evening bag."

Doc took his time in replying. Ivy could tell he was thinking. She soon found out just what he was thinking.

"Vivian told me she'd confided in you of our very long saga, and that included the moment we met in the malt shop. I must tell you the moment I set my eyes on Vivian, I knew she was the love of my life, although I never would have predicted the long road we took before being able to spend every moment together. I saw that look in that young man's eyes, Ivy. Loving someone doesn't take years. That spark can be lit in seconds."

"But I don't know a thing about him, Doc."

"All I knew about Vivian was she needed a place to sit down. The moment she did, I fell in love with her, and I'm even more in love with her today."

The train whistle blew. They were coming into the station.

Chapter Thirty

"Look, Ivy. Look at those three-standing outside in the cold waiting to greet us. They are in for a big surprise."

That big surprise was just waking up.

"Welcome to your new home, sleepyhead. Hold on now. Here we go," said Doc, as Ivy took the lead off the train. Staying back for a minute, Doc told Douglas to be ready.

"They're going to fall in love with you, Douglas." Pausing as he made his way down the few steps, Doc added, "Just like I have."

As Doc took the last step down onto the platform, he heard Elena let out one of her shrill screams.

"Look! Gramps is carrying a little reindeer!"

"Oh, be careful my love. Watch your step!"

"I will, Vivi. No problem."

Andy came to the rescue. "I'll take him, Grampa."

"I've got him, Andy. Move aside. Here comes Douglas!"

"Douglas! I love his name, Gramps!"

"Let's give him some room. We don't want Grampa to spend the night in the ER."

Vivian had prepared a late-night buffet. She thought they'd be wound up what with Walter not in his space in the barn. She hadn't planned on a little reindeer stealing the show once they got back to their barn. After smelling around and getting a sense of where things were and who was who, Douglas settled down with his blanket and rubber ball and fell sound asleep. He fit right in with the other reindeer.

"I'll leave the extra light on out here for a few nights until he gets his bearings," Doc explained as they all headed inside the house.

Vivian's buffet was just what they needed to calm down. Doc told the story of how it came to be that Noelene had chosen Doc to be Douglas's caretaker. He went even further.

"Douglas will belong to all of us. I'm not as spry as I was when Walter moved in."

"Don't worry, Gramps. I'll be here whenever I can be. I'm so happy Douglas came to stay with us. Walter would be happy too."

"Oh, you should have seen Walter watching the rabbits run around outside. He knew he was back in his barn. He knew his surroundings. You don't have to worry about Walter."

"But I still miss him, Gramps."

"That's because you love him, Elena. And you know who loved your reindeer decorations?"

"Who?"

"Noelene! I had my doubts whether or not she'd approve, but she loved the one Walter was wearing and thinks you are very caring of the animals and quite creative."

The conversation kept going, even after Vivian served her cinnamon swirl pumpkin pie with ice cream and coffee. Just before one, Ivy said good night.

"You are welcome to come New Year's Eve for dinner, although Doc and I aren't very exciting."

"Thanks, Vivian. I'll see where I'm at after I call Lawrence tomorrow. The busy season is getting underway."

It was snowing when Ivy headed home. She wasn't surprised.

Ivy had planned on doing some sketching, but she wasn't in the mood. Instead, she poured herself a glass of wine. Lighting a few candles, Ivy curled up on her old comfortable sofa and watched the snow coming down. Just as she was about to fall asleep, her phone rang. Ivy ignored it. Whoever it was tried again about twenty minutes later. This time Ivy got up to answer it. She worried something was wrong.

Before she could say a word, Vivian let her have it. "You never told me about the guy in the coffee shop!"

"I didn't think it was the time or the place."

"Well, there is no time like the present."

"There's not much to tell. I only spent about twenty minutes with him."

"Falling in love only takes a second."

"Doc told me the same thing. I never said I was in love, Vivian."

"Doc said he found your green velvet evening bag in a snowbank."

"His name is Nicholas."

"Why am I not surprised? When you think about it Ivy, Nicholas has been keeping hold of your heart since that awful night in Murphy's downtown hotel."

"What do you mean?"

"Doc said he found the velvet evening bag with the sweet little cranberry hearts the very night you lost it in the snow. Don't you find it ironic that after all those years, you run into him in a coffee shop, not a soda fountain, mind you, and he is the only person on the face of this earth to have found that velvet evening bag and you fall in love with him? What a beautiful love story, Ivy."

"For the sake of the story, let's say I did, as you say, fall in love with him. I hardly know him. I'll never see him again."

"Never is a cruel word. The universe is at work, young lady. Get a good night's sleep. This love story is just beginning."

After talking about and thinking about Nicholas, Ivy was wide awake. Taking a few candles with her upstairs, she filled the tub with hot water and soothing lavender bubble bath. Turning the light out, Ivy relaxed, watching the snow continue to fall.

Enjoying a bath was just what she needed after the trip with Doc and meeting Nicholas. Once she was in bed with her blankets and favorite quilt pulled up around her, Ivy fell sound asleep.

Those little birds at the feeders had Ivy up early again. Although she didn't get much sleep, it was a sound sleep. Ivy felt rested and ready for the new day. After making a pot of coffee, she brought a cup with her into her studio, where she immersed herself in the Elena Collection after writing down some points to discuss with Lawrence. She decided she'd head back to the city by the end of the week. The year ahead would be another busy one. She told herself to stay focused and try to avoid any talk of Nicholas with Vivian.

While I love her dearly, Vivian is a hopeless romantic.

With her coffee cup refilled, Ivy called Lawrence a few hours later. He updated her on where they stood with sales, coming shows and trips, the status of the Elena Collection, and most important, the wonderful news that he and Midge were expecting their first child come July.

"Congratulations, Lawrence! I am so happy for you."

"We are thrilled, Ivy. We haven't told too many. It is still early in the pregnancy, but I had to tell you since we plan on asking you to be this baby's godmother."

"Lawrence!"

It took Ivy a few seconds to gather her thoughts. After being focused on designs and fabrics, the worlds of babies and friendship took over the conversation.

"I am so honored you and Midge have chosen me to be your baby's godmother. I can't put into words what that means to me. Thank you, Lawrence. I will always be there for your child."

"I know that Ivy. You've always been there for me."

Before saying goodbye, they recapped what else they had discussed.

"Your calendar is filling up, Ivy. One thing I forgot to remind you about. Remember E. Jones from the *Times* called a while ago?"

"Yes. She was interested in interviewing me for a human-interest story."

"Right. She felt your story would be inspirational. Because she'd be heading your way to Vermont to do some skiing this coming week, she hoped to visit you at your farmhouse to do the interview. She'd be bringing along a *Times* photographer."

"When did we schedule her visit?"

"It's on the calendar for January second at eleven."

"I'll have to do some cooking."

"Well, you'll have to serve your meal in that original green velvet gown of yours because she asked if you could be wearing the dress. She wants to weave it into the story as well as take photos of you in it."

"I'll be up extra early doing some cooking."

After making decisions concerning the Elena Collection and confirming travel dates to events abroad, Ivy thanked Lawrence again for choosing her to be godmother to his first child.

When Ivy hung up the phone, she called Hazel. Ivy loved listening to Hazel's stories about her dolls and puzzles and drawings and hearing about Louise bothering her. Hazel enjoyed hearing Ivy's stories about when her mother was Louise's age and Ivy picked on her.

Touching base with Hazel put life into perspective.

"I love you, Aunt Ivy."

"I love you too, Hazel."

Those simple yet powerful few words always made Ivy smile.

After hanging up the phone, Ivy went online and ordered Hazel yet another doll with long hair to brush and braid and put pretty things in. She ordered Louise more stuffed animals, despite Izzie telling her Louise already had a bed full of them.

A girl can never have enough dolls with hair to style and stuffed animals to hug.

After her talk with Lawrence, Ivy realized she was behind in her work. She settled down and got organized, tuned out distractions, and played soft music or listened to the wind while working. Once focused, Ivy went to town. New Year's Eve didn't matter. She plowed right through it. By the next day, Ivy felt she was in pretty good shape. That's when she came up for air. That's when she remembered she had company coming the next day. She called Lawrence for suggestions of what to serve.

"Keep it simple," she advised. "I'll have to go to the store, and that's something I don't like to do. I'm not good at it. I can never find what I'm looking for."

"I'll make it easy. You can order a small platter of little sandwiches, each cut in half, with a plastic container full of sliced fruit from your grocery store. Or we can decide on a few simple dishes. From there, I'll make out a grocery list. Then I'll get a hold of the guy who buys your groceries and tell him you need everything on that list first thing in the morning. Keep in mind, E. Jones's focus is on your story, not on what you cook."

"Oh, Lawrence, I do love you. Let's pick out those recipes. I'll message you my caretaker's number. His name is Gerald. Tell him to please get here as early as possible. He will be rewarded."

By nine twenty the next morning, Ivy's home had the aroma of a five-star restaurant, or at least the diner where she worked years ago. Lawrence surprised her by overnighting tiramisu from his parents' restaurant. Just before she ran upstairs to get ready for her guests, Ivy gave Lawrence a quick call.

"Last night I told you I loved you, Lawrence. This morning I really, really love you. When I opened your package, all I could think about was that very cold and windy February day when you picked me up in a blizzard and took me to your parent's restaurant for the first time."

"I remember that day. They'd closed the restaurant but cooked us a great meal. We sat there for hours talking."

"You forgot to mention the wine we consumed and the tiramisu we enjoyed."

"What a life, Ivy. Let me know how it goes with E. Jones."

Chapter Thirty-One

CHECKING THE TIME, IVY HURRIED UPSTAIRS. Something told her the infamous reporter would not be late. By ten thirty, Ivy was coming down the stairs in her original green velvet gown. It felt rather quirky to be floating around the kitchen before noon dressed in velvet covered by an apron that was her grandmother's. Turning the music up, Ivy realized she enjoyed feeling quirky. It might have explained why she danced her way to the dining room table holding onto a casserole with flowered potholders. As she was lighting the candles, Ivy noticed an SUV coming down the driveway. Hurrying back to the kitchen, Ivy untied the apron, threw it in a drawer, and hustled back to open the door.

"Welcome to my retreat from the world. I hope you had good weather getting here."

"Not a problem. Not even one snowflake." E. Jones smiled, coming through the doorway. "You look lovely in your velvet dress, Ivy. Thank you for allowing us to intrude on your downtime. I know how precious that time can be. I'd like you to meet Robert Vinet, our photographer for the afternoon."

"It's very nice meeting you, Robert. I enjoy your work in the *Times*. Your photos pull me in every time."

"That explains why he's won so many awards."

"It certainly does," Ivy replied, noticing E. Jones was wearing her hair down. It went beyond her shoulders with highlights added. Eye makeup and a touch of lipstick gave her a softer, more feminine look. After dealing with models and brides, Ivy noticed such things.

Taking their coats, Ivy invited them into her home. Then the tour began. As they were going into the front room, Ivy asked E. Jones a question.

"It is none of my business, but I am a bit confused. Do I just call you E., or does the E stand for your name?"

"I appreciate you asking that question. Most people never ask. They just call me E. I don't tell many, but since you were kind enough to ask, my name is Esmeralda. It is a family name. I've never been able to wrap my head around it, so that's the reason for E. Jones. My mother still calls me Essie. You can too if you like."

"I love Essie for a name."

"I like it too, Ivy. But the readers would go haywire if I changed my byline at this point.'"

"I agree. So, what will be the angle of your story, Essie?"

"Everyone knows you are a highly successful wedding gown designer so I want to take them back to the beginning. I was enthralled when you told the story about the dress you are wearing. But I realize you have so many more chapters in your life to tell. I loved hearing about the desk your grandfather made for you and the time you went back as an adult to the house where you grew up. That alone is an inspirational story, Ivy. Most everyone has a house like that, kept close to their heart."

Essie made a suggestion. "Why don't we look around so Robert can get a sense of the surroundings and lighting."

Going into the den, Ivy pointed out the simple desk her grandfather made tucked underneath the bookshelves.

"Many of the books surrounding the desk were from my growing up years."

"So many books. You must have enjoyed reading."

"I still do, Essie, if I can find the time."

Robert decided the desk with Ivy sitting on the stool in her original green velvet dress would make an impactful photo. Once the first photo was taken, they relaxed a bit. It became less stressful. More natural. So as Robert did his thing and Ivy followed his instructions, E. Jones did the interview. They didn't finish until it was going on 3:30 p.m.

"I'm sure you're both tired and hungry. Please have a seat at the dining room table while I warm things up and pour us some wine."

"Need some help, Ivy?"

"No, I'm fine, Essie. I'm still learning about the kitchen and cooking. So far, so good."

"Whatever you've prepared, it smells delicious."

"Thanks, Robert. It is certainly nothing fancy."

As Ivy went to get wine glasses from a shelf in a pantry off the kitchen, feeling embarrassed that she forgot to put the glasses on the table in the first place, Ivy happened to look into the dining room just as Robert and Essie were kissing. They never noticed her. The kiss was a long one. Taking the glasses into the kitchen, Ivy filled them. Before serving the wine, she made some noise around the kitchen to let them know she was coming. It worked. They were sitting there, making note of the snow starting to fall.

"Do you have far to go tonight?"

"Not really," replied Robert, looking at Essie. "We're taking our time. We have ten days to get some skiing in."

Ivy's efforts in the kitchen paid off. Her guests enjoyed everything Ivy served. Lawrence's tiramisu was a hit, as was the coffee served with it. When the grandfather clock in the front hall announced the seven o'clock hour, Essie nudged Robert.

"I didn't realize the time. We'd best get on the road. It's dark out and still snowing."

"You're welcome to stay here. I have plenty of room."

"I appreciate your offer, Ivy, but we'll be fine." Essie smiled.

After a quick wrap-up covering the story, the photos, and a timeline, Ivy went for their coats.

"Thank you for opening up your beautiful farmhouse to us and for being so generous with your time and for preparing such a delicious supper. I am thrilled we were able to spend time together in such a relaxed setting. Nothing against New York, if you know what I mean."

"I know what you mean, Essie. I had so much fun with the two of you. I've been interviewed and photographed many times, but this was the best."

"Save that thought until you see the results," joked Robert, running outside to clean the car off and get it started.

When he came back in, he thanked Ivy for a wonderful time.

"Now E. Jones, we better get going while we can."

"Take your time. If it's too bad, turn around and spend the night."

Ivy watched their headlights until they disappeared.

Leaving the porch light on in case they did return, Ivy decided to get things cleaned up before she went to bed. After blowing out the candles in the dining room, she figured it'd be best to get changed before getting started. Doing dishes in a velvet dress just wouldn't work. As Ivy started up the stairs, a noise of some kind outside caught her attention. She knew enough not to open the door. Critters loved roaming around in the dark. Pulling the curtains in the front room back, she saw nothing going on except for the snow still falling. That noise was getting a little louder. Ivy stayed still. The more she listened, the more she realized there was a rhythm to that noise. Ivy slowly opened the door. The noise became louder. Stepping onto the front porch with a Christmas wreath still in place now covered in snow, Ivy caught sight of what looked like someone standing off in the snow. To her amazement, this person was playing a harmonica. Something told her to keep going. There was nothing to fear.

Down the snowy steps she went with her slippers on. Standing there in her original green velvet gown, the slight wind moving her auburn hair, it dawned on Ivy that she was listening to a harmonica playing "Silent Night." Her heart quickened.

"Before you leave me, tell me your favorite song."

Nicholas's words came dancing through the snowflakes.

And then, as she looked through those glittering snowflakes, there stood Nicholas, playing a harmonica, playing that favorite song. There, with a smile as warm as sunshine, stood the man who stole her heart in a coffee shop up in the mountains.

Ivy was certain she heard that philharmonic off in the wind when he said her name, gently, lovingly.

"I finally found you, Ivy Nolan."

The wind kept it up, creating those snowy little whirlwinds, sending them across the fields as Nicholas kept playing, kept moving toward Ivy.

Once back by her side, Nicholas took Ivy's hand. "Would you like to dance, my love?"

There was no hesitation.

The song of that wind with snowflakes falling and bare tree limbs moving brought the two together on that January eve. Pulling her close, Nicholas wrapped Ivy up in his arms and slowly, very slowly, they moved to the rhythm of nature's song under glistening snowflakes.

Pushing stands of auburn hair away from her eyes, Nicholas whispered as the sound of a train going down a track only heightened their emotions.

"I love you, Ivy. I never want to let you go."

"A dear friend of mine told me falling in love only takes a second. I believe that with all my heart. I love you, Nicholas, now and forever."

They kept dancing. They weren't cold. They just kept dancing.

"You play the harmonica beautifully."

"You look stunning in your green velvet gown."

"I normally don't wear it around the house. It's a long story."

"I'm eager to create our own stories, Ivy."

"And what would you call our first story, my love?"

Pulling Ivy even closer, swirling them about the beauty of winter, Nicholas whispered, "I would call our first story 'velvet snowflakes.'"

It was snowing even harder.

In the distance reindeer pranced.

Velvet snowflakes kept falling and falling.

Ivy Nolan's
Banana Bread

IN THE STORY, IVY BAKES WARMLY spiced cinnamon swirl banana bread using her grandmother's banana bread recipe to serve guests invited for dinner. It's a family favorite, included in Christmas gatherings over the years.

Luckily, like Ivy, our family still has my grandmother's banana bread recipe. This recipe is near and dear to our hearts. In fact, it was the first recipe my daughter Natalie learned to make when she began baking! Natalie has since started the popular baking blog *Parsley and Icing*. Fittingly, Natalie's great-grandmother's banana bread (with an added cinnamon swirl) was one of the first recipes on *Parsley and Icing*!

We invite you to visit Natalie's website, parsleyandicing.com, for this beloved cinnamon swirl banana bread recipe as well as many other original dessert recipes.

Ivy Nolan's Sour Cream Chocolate Chip Cookies

On Christmas Eve, Ivy's family gathers at her home. The dinner is catered, yet being that it's Christmas, Ivy has baked a batch of cookies ahead of time. Ivy's sour cream chocolate chip cookie recipe is adapted from one of her grandmother's recipes.

This was another one of the first recipes my daughter Natalie made when she started her food blog. Ivy (and Natalie) add chocolate chips to these classic sour cream cookies. You can get Ivy's cookie recipe at parsleyandicing.com.

We hope these cookies will be a part of your family's holiday baking traditions as well.

BARBARA BRIGGS WARD IS A WRITER living in Ogdensburg, New York. Her short story "The Kitchens" was third runner-up in *The Saturday Evening Post's* 2021 Great American Fiction Contest. She is the author of a beloved Christmas trilogy for adults featuring *The Reindeer Keeper*, (chosen by Yahoo!'s Christmas Books Club as their December 2012 Book of the Month), *The Snowman Maker* and *The Candle Giver*. Other works of fiction include *The Tin Cookie Cutter* and *A Robin's Snow*. Her short stories have appeared in three *Chicken Soup for the Soul* books and *Highlights* for Children. Her essay centered around her grandmother was one of eight essays selected to appear in Ladies Home Journal, July 1976, highlighting women who represent the "Real Beauties of America." Barbara's feature on Boldt Castle was published in McCall's. She has been a featured author on Mountain Lake PBS and Target Book Festivals in Boston and New York. For more, visit barbarabriggsward.com.

JOHN MORROW WAS BORN IN OGDENSBURG, NY in 1948. Spending much of his childhood in the Buffalo area, he returned to Ogdensburg in 1971 and was an art instructor at Ogdensburg Free Academy, until retiring in 2003.

Working in watercolor, oil and acrylic, much of the theme of his art is a relationship between nature, man, and time. The style of his work will often vary to express the characteristics of his subject. He works from a variety of sources including sketches, photographs and memory, often editing by deleting elements or adding them until he is satisfied with the compo-

sition. He has studied and been influenced over the years by the work of Andrew Wyeth, Richard Schmid, Edward Hooper, and The Hudson River School painters.

Over the past several decades, John's work has been shown in hundreds of shows and exhibitions and used on the cover of several book and magazines including the cover of *Reader's Digest*. John and his wife Brenda continue to live in the St. Lawrence Valley that is rich in history and artistic subject matter. You can view his gallery at:

https://jmorrow.com/

CPSIA information can be obtained
at www.ICGtesting.com
Printed in the USA
BVHW042209251022
650311BV00001B/12